YOU RUINED ME

ISABEL JORDAN

ALSO BY ISABEL JORDAN

CONTEMPORARY ROMANCE/ROMANTIC COMEDY

You Complicate Me

You Wrecked Me

You Ruined Me

The Has-Been and the Hot Mess

PARANORMAL ROMANCE

The Harper Hall Investigations series reading order:

Semi-Charmed

Semi-Human

Semi-Twisted

Semi-Broken

Semi-Sane

Semi-Obsessed

Semi-Magical

The Harper Hall Investigations complete series boxset

SUPERHERO ROMANCE

Caped and Dangerous

For all the fans out there who asked, "When are we getting Michael's story???"—then were patient with me when I answered, "What? Why???" You all were right. This one's for you.

CHAPTER 1

*N*othing screamed "pathetic" like buying a gallon of cheap vodka at an IGA on a weekday afternoon in the hopes of getting so *trashed* you forgot your ex-fiancée was marrying your douchebag cousin. In two days.

But *knowing* it was pathetic didn't stop Michael Montgomery from putting the vodka in his cart. Or the four pints of Ben and Jerry's. Or the party-sized bag of Cheetos. Or the clearance 12-pack of Reese's peanut butter pumpkins that had clearly been sitting on the shelf since Halloween three months ago.

At least he wasn't still heartbroken. He could only *imagine* what kind of fuckery he'd be up to if he was still in love with Sadie.

It'd taken a while, but he was completely over her. Hell, he was *almost* happy she was ass-over-elbow in love with his douchebag cousin, Gage.

No, it wasn't his wounded heart or pride that'd led him to the dark, carb-tastic place he was wallowing in at the moment.

What was currently driving him to drink (and probably put himself at risk for diabetes) was the thought of showing up to the wedding and having everyone *else* looking at him, feeling sorry for him, giving him the oh-poor-Michael-got-dumped-for-his-better-looking-and-more-successful-douchebag-cousin head tilt.

He *hated* that head tilt.

He'd been getting it ever since Sadie left him at the alter six years ago. It'd gotten worse when she and Gage announced their engagement last year.

It also didn't help that he'd be flying completely solo at this thing. He hadn't had a girlfriend in...shit, had it been two years?

Yep. It'd been two years since Katie dumped him. Turned out, she'd been expecting an engagement ring for Christmas, so the Bath and Body Works gift card he'd given her had been about as well received as a raging case of syphilis.

He still had a tiny little dent over his right eyebrow from where she'd flung the gift card holder at him.

The moral of the story was, never disappoint a marriage-minded dental hygienist who'd pitched for her college softball team.

Anything more than casual sex lost its appeal to him after The Katie Incident. Which was fine...until he needed a wedding date and had absolutely *no one* he could fathom taking to such a thing.

Michael sighed and threw a box of Lucky Charms into his cart. He wandered over to the produce aisle, wondering idly if some kale would help cancel out the damage he was about to do to his body with alcohol and sugar.

That's when he saw *her*.

It wasn't her beauty that grabbed his attention. (Though, he'd admit, she was *definitely* cute in a curvy, girl-next-door way.) It was the look of absolute, stricken horror on her face as she stared up at the guy who'd just approached her.

Michael casually moved in closer and pretended to be scoping out the organic bananas so that he could hear what was going on. He might not be much of a gentleman (Katie would certainly testify to *that*) but he wasn't going to let some poor woman get harassed in the produce aisle. Not on his watch.

The woman gulped and twisted her mouth up into the most painful fake smile Michael had ever seen as she looked up into the guy's face. She shifted the plastic bag of limes she was white knuckling to her cart and ran a shaky hand over her hair.

"Oh, Steve...hi. It's so *good* to see you," she said.

Oh, it was so *not* good to see Steve, Michael thought. The look on her face *clearly* said seeing him was as pleasant as having her insides carved out with a rusty spoon.

Steve's smile was far less forced, but there was something about it that made Michael want to punch the guy. He was smarmy. Used car salesman-y. And he looked kind of like a breathing Ken doll—plastic, phony, and overly coiffed.

"Dee," Steve said, his voice brimming with syrupy sympathy. "I'm glad I ran into you. You know, I just felt *terrible* about how everything went down last time we talked. You *have* to know I *never* wanted to hurt you like that."

Ah. Now it was making sense. Steve and this woman—Dee —had dated. And apparently, Steve had been a colossal dick to her when they stopped dating. Shocking.

Michael shifted his gaze back to Dee. She looked like she wanted the floor to open up and swallow her whole.

Her thick auburn hair was piled on top of her head in a messy bun that looked so precarious, a deep sigh would topple it. There didn't appear to be much makeup on her face, because he could see the light smattering of freckles that dotted her little button nose from where he stood.

And her outfit…well, that could only be described as *chaotic*.

Dee was wearing a white tank top with Kylo Ren holding out a Valentine's Day card to Rey and the words "I've Ben Solo for too long" printed across her breasts. That was topped off with the slouchiest gray cardigan Michael had ever seen, accented by baggy pink sweatpants with holes in them, and fur-lined boots that came up to her knees.

Michael wasn't an expert on women. He'd never, *ever* claim to know what they were thinking. But even *he* knew *this* was not what a woman wanted to look like when she saw her smarmy, khaki-and-pressed-golf-shirt-wearing ex-boyfriend.

Dee licked her lips and let out a thin laugh. "Oh, its fine, Steve. Really. We don't need to talk about all that."

She moved in front of her cart, obviously trying to block it from Steve's view. Out of curiosity, Michael took a peek.

Tequila, limes, economy bag of chocolate chips, Pop Tarts, Pringles, and two jumbo boxes of tampons.

He winced in sympathy. Dee was *not* having a good day.

Michael could relate on just about every conceivable level.

"I need to, though," Steve said, giving her the sympathetic head tilt that Michael knew all too well. The fucker. "I want to make sure you realize that Sherry and I…well, we never meant for anything to happen. We just fell in *love*. I mean, the heart wants what the heart wants, you know?"

Michael was pretty sure he puked in his mouth a little. Jesus. What a fucking tool. Dee had actually had *sex* with this guy? Yikes.

"No, really, Steve, we don't need to talk about it," Dee said dryly.

Michael had to swallow a chuckle. She was down, but not

out, he realized. There was still plenty of fight in her. He really admired that.

But that's when everything went all pear-shaped.

A tall, scrawny blonde dressed in a red scrap of fabric that Michael was pretty sure was a handkerchief (because *holy hell* who would make a *dress* in that size) sidled up to Steve and snaked her arm through his.

Sherry, Michael presumed.

"They're all out of condoms, babe," Sherry said, then ran her eyes over Dee, from the tips of her messy hair, down to the toes of her furry boots. Sherry's smile was *not* kind. "Oh, hi, Dee. I didn't even see *you* there."

Dee visibly swallowed three times as she looked up at Sherry, then shifted her gaze to where the other woman's arm was touching Steve's. Her eyes—her huge, misty gray eyes—looked suspiciously glassy, like she was in danger of bursting into tears at any second.

Yeah, *that* wasn't going to happen.

Without bothering to come up with a plan, Michael abandoned his cart and threw himself right into the fray.

This was either going to be totally heroic...or a complete train wreck he'd regret for the rest of his life.

But, hey, you only live once, right?

CHAPTER 2

*D*elilah Morgenstern was silently contemplating whatever she might've done to piss off Karma when the handsome stranger draped his arm over her shoulders and grinned down at her like she was the best thing he'd seen all night.

She was dead, wasn't she? She'd died of mortification after seeing Steve and the skank he'd cheated on her with at the fucking IGA while she was wearing a *Star Wars* T-shirt and yesterday's sweatpants, and now a hot guy was here to take her to heaven—or hell.

Could go either way, she supposed. She was generally a decent person, but she *had* stolen that lipstick from Walgreens when she was ten. So, if God was *really* a stickler for that whole "thou shalt not steal" thing, she imagined Hot Guy was about to take her on the express elevator down to The Bad Place.

Which, honestly, would be better than standing *here*, pretending that seeing Steve and Sherry together wasn't like having a rabid dog rip into her gut and eat her liver.

"Did you get everything, hon?" Hot Guy asked her. "Ready to go?"

Hon. Hot Guy called her hon. What kind of fucked up fever dream was she *having* right now?

"Um...yeah," she said. "I, uh, think I have everything."

Obviously she'd been rendered stupid by how good his warm, solid arm felt across her shoulders...and by how he looked a little like the love child of Captain America and The Winter Soldier.

He smelled good, too. Like laundry detergent, antibacterial soap, and sunshine. She probably smelled like the two-day-old Chinese leftovers she'd scarfed before heading out for more depression supplies.

But Hot Guy didn't seem to care as he tugged her a little closer and tucked her protectively against his side. He shifted his warm, whiskey-brown eyes over to Steve and stuck his hand out.

"Hi," he said. "Michael Montgomery. And you are?"

A furrow developed between Steve's perfectly waxed eyebrows as he sized Hot Guy—no, *Michael*—up.

Delilah understood the furrow. Steve had accused her of letting herself go when he broke up with her. And now, here was a stupid-hot guy at her side, looking down at her like she *belonged* next to him.

Wait...why *was* he at her side, looking down at her like she belonged next to him? With her luck, this whole thing was going to end with her as the star of an unsolved mystery on *Dateline.*

"Steve Connell," he said, taking Michael's hand. "And this is my girlfriend, Sherry."

Sherry's eyes traveled over Michael like he was a piece of

tiramisu at a 5-star restaurant. "Charmed," she murmured, touching the tip of her tongue to her upper lip.

Delilah wanted to rip that tongue out and shove it up Sherry's surgically altered nose. Or up Steve's ass.

Yeah, that'd work just as well.

Meanwhile, Michael and Steve seemed to be doing that handshake-of-death thing men did when they wanted to piss all over their territory.

Having a penis must be *exhausting*, Delilah thought.

Given the way Steve flexed his fingers when they finally let go of each other's hand, she'd say Michael won that round. Ha!

Steve asked, "And how do you know our little Dee, Michael?"

Delilah winced. At five-foot-three, she didn't need anyone to remind her she was *little*. Plus, she *hated* it when Steve called her Dee. Like *Delilah* was just too many syllables to remember? Or like he was just too lazy to use her whole name?

Michael glanced down at her again, and one corner of his mouth quirked up. "Oh, we go *way* back."

A nervous burst of hyena-like laughter spilled out of Delilah's mouth under the force of all that hotness being directed down at her. This was so surreal! This was either *The Twilight Zone*, or she was tripping from that one time in 9th grade when Ally Sherber convinced her to try shrooms.

Her mom—and McGruff the crime dog—told her that night would come back to haunt her when she least expected it.

She should've listened.

Sherry tipped her head to one side and narrowed her eyes on Michael. Delilah could practically *feel* the disbelief rolling off her in waves. "So, you're what? Like, just a friend?"

Sherry's tone implied *"Because a sloppy cow like her couldn't possibly be dating a god like you."* But she didn't outright say it.

Probably because *Sherry* was currently banging someone who used to bang Delilah on a regular basis. Although not usually in a mutually satisfying manner.

But *that* was another story for another time.

Michael looked Sherry up and down, and his eyes went cold. Sherry probably wasn't used to that. Delilah enjoyed the *hell* out of the surprise on the bitch's face when she realized she'd been judged and found lacking.

"Oh, there's nothing *just friends* about our relationship," Michael said, letting his hand fall over her shoulder enough that if she took a deep breath, his fingertips would be on her breast.

Holy Dollywood!

Her skin suddenly felt three sizes too small and her nipples were so hard someone could lose an eye if they tripped and fell into her.

She looked up at Steve and watched that furrow in his brow deepen. He was obviously doing the mental math on just how long "way back" was. He was wondering if *she'd* been cheating on *him* with Michael while *he* was cheating on *her* with Sherry.

Ha! Let him stew on that for a while. Served the jackass right.

It was *especially* satisfying that Michael was way hotter than Steve.

Steve was good looking in a corporate accountant, vanilla kind of way. His jawline was a little soft, his skin a little pasty, his body lean but not at all muscle-y. He could best be described as average. Average height, average build.

There was nothing *average* about Michael.

His short hair was on the darkest possible end of the blond family, and his cheekbones were sharp enough to etch glass. He had a strong jaw, too. Like strong enough to take one hell of a punch.

Not that she'd punch him. She'd never do anything to mess up *that* face. The point was, he had a really manly, chiseled jaw.

And he was tall. The top of Delilah's head only came up to his armpit. Michael was several inches taller than Steve, so he was, what, probably six two? Six three?

And this god-among-men had picked *her* out of the supermarket and made her his good deed of the day? Out of the kindness of his heart?

Yeah, no. Her luck didn't run like that. He must have an ulterior motive, and she didn't want *anything* to do with it. Her life was tragic enough as it was, thank you very much. Time to cut this debacle short.

Delilah moved out from under Michael's arm (damn, it was cold without his body heat at her side) and grabbed his hand, tugging him toward the register while steering her cart with her free hand. "Steve, Sherry, it was nice seeing you, but we have to go. Now."

"Yeah, uh, yeah, sure, Dee…" Steve muttered, sounding as dazed as she felt. "We'll talk again soon," he promised. Or threatened. It certainly felt more like a threat to Delilah.

"Come on, babe," Sherry said through gritted teeth, tugging on his sleeve.

Michael grinned lazily down at Delilah and said in a ridiculously loud stage whisper, "Too bad about the condoms. I guess we'll have to stop somewhere else on the way home."

Someone made a choking sound. It might have been her.

Seriously, Karma, what did I ever do to you?

CHAPTER 3

*S*he stayed silent until they got to the register, but Michael could practically *hear* her thoughts. *That's how hard she was concentrating on holding herself together.*

As they got in line behind a lady who looked to be buying two of every brand of cat food in the place, she let go of his hand and glared up at him.

The first thing Michael noticed was that she was even prettier when she was angry. That was really saying something, too, because she was *damn* pretty, even with the fake smile she'd been giving Steve.

And secondly...would it be weird if he grabbed her hand again? She had the softest skin he'd ever felt.

She smacked his chest with the back of her hand. "What the hell, man? What *was* that?"

Michael shoved a hand through his hair. Shit. He *had* taken some liberties that bordered on sexual harassment. "I'm sorry. It just looked like you could use some help back there. And that douchebag just looked so...smug." He shrugged apologetically.

"I don't know. I just couldn't stand to see him and Dance Club Skank Barbie treat you like that, I guess."

Her lower lip twitched. "Dance Club Skank Barbie?"

Another sheepish shrug. "If the painted on spandex fits."

She wanted to smile. He could see it. But she held herself back for some reason. Then she asked, "Why do you care?"

It wasn't a snarky question. She sounded genuinely curious as to why he'd defend a stranger. He wished he had an answer that didn't make him sound like a pathetic loser. But, since he didn't, he said, "Look, I'm having a shitty week. You looked like you were having a shitty week, too. I guess I felt, I don't know, some kind of kinship. An us-against-them thing, you know?"

She licked her lips and Michael wasn't proud of how his eyes involuntarily tracked the motion like a hungry wolf trailing a hapless baby bunny through the woods.

It'd obviously been *way* too long since he'd gotten laid.

Then she bit down on that lush lower lip of hers and he fought back a groan. She was *killing* him and had absolutely no idea.

"It was *kind of* the coolest thing anyone has ever done for me," she admitted quietly.

"Yeah?"

"Yeah."

Well, that was just sad. Who had she been hanging out with that such a minor thing was considered the coolest thing ever? But also…it made him feel very manly in a totally Tarzan-saves-Jane, caveman kind of way.

Again, not something he was especially proud of.

"I'm glad I was able to help," he said gruffly.

When cat food lady was finally checked out and ready to leave, Michael loaded her groceries onto the conveyor belt and gave Dee a sharp look when she tried to give the cashier her credit card. He handed his own over before she could object.

"Thank you," she said, exasperated. "Again."

Michael looked past her to see Steve and Sherry heading toward the registers, still watching them closely. He lifted his chin in their direction. "They've still got an eye on you. They'll know something's up if we leave in different cars. Should we stall until they're gone?"

She glanced out into the parking lot. "Well, did you have plans for the evening?"

He'd planned to get drunk off his ass and binge watch *Cobra Kai* on Netflix. But he didn't really see the need to divulge *that*. "No. Not really."

"There's a diner across the street that makes the best waffles I've ever had. We could walk over there and have breakfast for dinner." She glanced down at her watch. "Or, late lunch, I guess. What do you call that? Linner? Dunch?"

She was blushing down to the roots of her hair, which he found absolutely adorable. Was she afraid he was going to say no to her? After all this? "I'm buying," she tacked on quickly.

Yeah, not happening. "I'd love to, Dee."

She let out a deep breath and said, "OK. That's great. But only Steve calls me Dee and I *hate* it. My name's Delilah."

"Oh, hey there—"

She held up a hand. "If you say, 'hey there, Delilah' or ask me what it's like in New York City, I'm going to have to nut-punch you. That fucking song ruined every introduction I've had to new people since 2006."

He scoffed. "I wasn't going to say that."

Except he'd *totally* been about to say that. Who wouldn't?

"It's nice to meet you, Delilah," he said, realizing just how much better the beautiful name suited her than the shortened version.

Then she did something he hadn't seen her do yet—not for real, anyway. She smiled, wide and bright, and it lit up the room like the sun.

Why did he suddenly get the feeling he was in *way* over his head with this one?

They were doing God's work at the Harlen Street Diner. Angels were obviously in the kitchen, making waffles according to God's own personal recipe.

That was Delilah's story, and she was sticking to it.

She couldn't hold back a moan as she forked up another bite. "That's so good," she mumbled around her mouthful of crispy, sweet, angelically wonderful deliciousness. "Didn't I tell you?"

Michael paused with his fork halfway to his mouth as he watched her eat her body weight in carbs. "Yeah, you told me," he said, eyes on her mouth, sounding distracted.

He was probably amazed by the sheer amount of food she could put away. She was pretty sure that in another life, she'd been a Hobbit. There were just too many similarities for it not to be true. (Her lack of height, her love of breakfast, second breakfast, elevenses, lunch, afternoon tea, dinner and supper. And of course, there were the occasional stray hairs she had to shave off her toes. But she saw no need to mention any of *that* to the hot guy sitting across from her. Especially not the hairy toes. Ahem.)

Steve sometimes tried to order her a salad when they went out. She always nixed that and ordered whatever the hell she wanted. But it still hurt enough that over the last six months or so, she'd stopped eating in front of him at all.

But Michael didn't look disgusted while he watched her eat, so she decided to ignore it. "So, you said at the store that you were having a shitty week. What happened?"

He was quiet for a second while he chewed and swallowed his own bite of waffle.

His waffle manners were *much* better than hers, she decided. Just one more thing he looked better than her doing. If he hadn't saved her from epic embarrassment, she'd probably hate him for being so damned perfect.

Eventually, he said, "I have to go watch my ex-fiancée marry my cousin this weekend."

She almost sucked syrup directly into her lungs with her gasp of sympathy. "Your fiancée dumped you for your cousin? And you have to go to the wedding? What kind of bullshit is that?"

He raised a brow at her. "How do you know *she* dumped *me*? Maybe I dumped her."

Delilah sucked air through her teeth. "Dude, look, no offense intended, but I met you at a supermarket, you had no plans for the evening, and I saw the cart you abandoned. You had ice cream, Cheetos, and vodka—which is almost as bad as what I was buying." She gestured to his chest with her fork. "Plus there's a ketchup stain on your Henley and you're wearing gray sweatpants. Welcome to Dumpsville, my friend—population, *us*."

She wouldn't mention that while she looked like a hobo in her depression uniform, he was *fuck* hot in a stained Henley and sweats. Bastard.

He snorted. "Rude," he said without heat. "Correct, but rude."

She shrugged. "I figured we were at the point in our super-weird acquaintance where we could be honest with each other. So, why'd she dump you?"

He set his fork down and pushed his sleeves up. She refused —absolutely *refused*—to notice how nice his forearms were. "We were too young and stupid to get married," he said. "She just realized it before I did. It was the right call."

"And the cousin?"

"They didn't hook up until five years later. I wasn't wronged in any way." He rubbed a hand over his scruffy jaw. "Gage and Sadie belong together. I'm happy for them."

Well, he was *definitely* a better person than she was. Because if Steve dumped her for anyone in her family, she'd be studying up on voodoo so that she could make sure he never got his dick up again.

Hell, now that her mind had gone *there*, she might do a little Googling on the subject when she got home. Couldn't hurt to try, right? "Why the vodka and Cheetos binge then?"

He rested his really nice forearms on the table and narrowed his eyes on her. "You ask a lot of questions."

She swallowed her last bite of waffle, which made her idly wonder if there was anything sadder in the world than an empty plate, then set her fork down with a sigh. "Already clamming up on me, fake boyfriend? That's gotta be a record for 'shortest relationship ever.'"

Michael chuckled. "I guess I'm not as depressed about seeing her get married as I am about being so far away from that kind of love myself, you know? My luck with romance has been tragic."

Delilah shot him skeptical side eye. "Sure it has. Whatever you say, pal."

He raised a brow at her, which was just another thing that

irritated her. She couldn't raise just one eyebrow, and when she tried, it looked like she was having a stroke.

"Why the skepticism?" he asked.

She swirled her index finger around to gesture to, well, *all* of him. "I mean, look at you. How bad can it have been for someone like you? That hair, that bone structure, that body...I seriously question whether any of you Prom King types ever had it *half* as bad as all the normal folk."

Michael snorted and let out a deep bark of laughter that snagged the attention of every ovary in the room, hers included. "I hate to shit all over your little theory, but I was *not* Prom King. Far from it, my friend. I was a nerd with a capital Dungeons and Dragons."

She crossed her arms over her chest. Now he was just messing with her. "*You* were a nerd. Like, honor student nerd?" Because she'd seen plenty of straight-A students who'd incorrectly labeled themselves as nerds over the years, and it was just an insult to *actual* nerds everywhere.

He looked her right in the eye and said, "Chess club."

"That's nothing," she scoffed. "I was president of the *AV* club."

He looked vaguely impressed right before he said, "Marching band. Trumpet."

She narrowed her eyes on him. "Tuba."

In fact, she still had freakishly strong biceps from hauling that thing around all through high school. Even with all his muscles, she was pretty sure she could wipe the floor with him in an arm-wrestling match.

"Class treasurer," he said, a challenging glint in his eyes.

Pfffttt. Amateur. "Voted most likely to spend time learning to speak Klingon *and* most likely to get arrested for stalking George Lucas," she shot back.

"Well, do you? Speak Klingon, that is?"

"*Wo' batlhvaD!*" she barked out, her sharp Klingon inflection startling a kid at the next table into dropping his fork on the floor. She shot his now-glaring mother an apologetic smile.

For the glory of the empire, she'd said.

No reason to admit that back in high school, she'd purchased and practically memorized an English-to-Klingon dictionary.

Michael looked suitably impressed as he leaned back in his chair. "Nice. But like I said, I was far from the Prom King type. I am, to this day, 100% nerd and proud."

She just wasn't sure how he could say that with a straight face while he sat there looking like *that*. "To this day, huh?"

"Try me."

Oh, now it was *on*.

"Fine," she said, giving him what she was sure was an evil, Grinch-y smile. "List every Star Wars film, ranked best to worst without looking anything up online."

His answering smile shot straight to her panties, which made her cross her legs. Hard.

He never broke eye contact or even blinked as he answered, "*The Empire Strikes Back*, obviously. Then, by a narrow margin, *The Last Jedi*. After that, it's *A New Hope, Return of the Jedi, The Force Awakens, Revenge of the Sith, The Phantom Menace, Rogue One, Solo, Attack of the Clones. The Rise of Skywalker* is dead last, and I'd nuke it from orbit if I could." Then he gave her the sexiest smirk she'd ever seen in her life, and said, "Well? Based on those answers, did I pass your nerd test?"

Based on those answers, she'd marry him and have his babies. But that was beside the point. She sniffed. "You did OK."

The glint in his eye told her he *knew* he'd done better than just OK. Cocky, sexy, nerd *bastard*.

"What about you?" he asked. "Do I get to test *your* nerd knowledge?"

Glad for a distraction from his all-around sexiness, she said, "Bring it on, Poindexter."

"If you were going to report to duty on the Enterprise, who would you want your captain to be?" he asked.

Oh, she was a little ashamed to admit she'd given this particular question *way* too much thought. "Well, Janeway, obviously."

He grunted. "Because she's a woman? Girl power and all that?"

"This isn't about gender equality at *all*, and frankly I'm a little insulted you'd think I'd go there. Look, Kirk was a lot of fun, but he was also a crazy, reckless bastard and would've probably got me killed, so I wouldn't pick him. Picard was pretty great, but he lost all rationality when it came to the Borg, so I wouldn't pick him. Sisco played it *way* too safe, so he's out. Janeway was the perfect blend of daring and caution. She's the only choice that makes any sense."

He looked a little stunned. She was a little stunned, too. She'd spit all that out in one breath.

"What about Archer?" Michael finally asked.

She frowned. "I always forget he exists. I liked his dog, though. That Beagle was freakin' adorable."

There was that sexy grin again. "Same. And agree about the dog."

Delilah took a sip of her hot chocolate and glanced up at him from underneath her lashes. Suddenly feeling a little shy, since she'd basically just flashed all her nerd knowledge at him at once. She usually got to know someone a little better before letting them see all *that*. "So, I guess we're both giant nerds, huh?"

"Yep. Definitely."

"Well, you don't *look* like a nerd."

His answering smile was wickedly hot. "Neither do you."

Delilah knew in that moment that she'd found a unicorn. A stupid-hot, smart, kind guy who looked like he could model in expensive cologne commercials and on billboards for designer boxer briefs in his spare time.

She was *so* in over her head with this one.

CHAPTER 4

Michael finished off his coffee and watched as Delilah did the same with her hot chocolate. He started to feel an empty, gnawing ache in his gut, which was super weird since he'd just eaten a month's worth of waffles. Then he realized what it was.

They were done with their meal, Steve and Sherry were long gone, and he was out of excuses to continue his fake date with Delilah.

He didn't want to leave her. She was so easy to talk to. And look at. He'd be happy to just sit and watch her eat, frankly. The joy on her face and in her beautiful eyes as she enjoyed her food was a turn on. A big one.

He'd never gotten hard watching a woman eat...until tonight.

"What do you do for a living, Michael?" she asked.

That was another turn on. Her voice. It was low-pitched and a little raspy. Totally sexy. And the way his name sounded on her lips...

He shifted uncomfortably in his seat and gave himself a sharp mental slap across the face. This *wasn't* a date. She *wasn't* his real girlfriend, and they would *not* be going back to his place to have sex, no matter what he'd said in front of Steve and Sherry. He had no business thinking about how she'd sound moaning his name as he grabbed her hips and slid his...

Another mental slap. Jesus. He needed to get his shit together. "I'm an art teacher at Vasilly Academy."

Her brows rose into her hairline. "How very upper crust-y of you."

He snorted. "My sister says the same thing, but she'll be happy when her daughter is old enough to go there and I can get her in. What about you?"

"Vasilly Academy would never take me," she said. "I'm a trailer park kid." Then her eyes widened. "Oh, you meant what do *I* do for a living, didn't you?"

Fuck, she was adorable. "Yes, Delilah. That's what I meant."

"I'm a photographer. Weddings, family portraits, graduation photos...that sort of thing."

He could've guessed by looking at her that she was, like him, a creative type. Maybe that explained the damn-near instant chemistry he'd felt with her.

They made small talk for a few more minutes, then he practically had to wrestle her to get the bill out of her hand when their waitress dropped it off. She was strong, he'd give her that. But he was faster, and ultimately, that's what got him to the register before her with his credit card in hand.

And now, as he walked her to her car, his mind was racing a million miles an hour. He could just ask her out, he supposed. He'd be busy this weekend with all the wedding nonsense, but after that...maybe.

Next to him, Delilah rifled through her ginormous handbag,

then triumphantly produced a *Ren & Stimpy* key chain that made him smile.

He could kiss her, he realized. She was so close. All he had to do was lean down just a little and…

No. Was he *insane*? He couldn't kiss a woman he'd just met. She'd think he was a psycho. He had to play this cool or else he'd scare her off for good.

She smiled up at him. "It was really nice to meet you, Michael. I had a lot of fun tonight."

"Come home with me," he blurted.

D'oh!

So much for playing it cool, jackass.

Her eyes widened. "Uh…"

He held up a hand. "That came out wrong. I meant, this has been a lot of fun, and I'd hate for it to end so soon. I mean, we have plenty of tequila. We were both planning to get drunk tonight, anyway. We could go back to my place, drink, and watch movies or something."

That was the lamest pitch in the history of lame pitches. But he was desperate. Something in his gut was telling him not to let her go. Not yet, anyway.

She licked her lips. "Michael, I'd like that, but you're still a stranger. It wouldn't be smart for me to go home with a stranger."

So, it wasn't that she didn't *like* him. She was just afraid he'd turn out to be a sicko or something.

He could work with that.

"OK," he began, "we can go to your place. You can drive. You can take my picture before we get in the car and send it, along with my driver's license number, to as many friends as you want. That way, everyone knows you're with me. What kind of guy with bad intentions would be that transparent?"

She was wavering. He could see it. He reached out and tucked a wayward strand of hair behind her ear, letting his fingertips brush her cheek. "If you say no," he said, "I totally understand. No hard feelings. And I'll still ask you to go out with me again after the wedding next weekend. But...I'm just not ready to say goodbye to you for some reason."

Delilah sucked in a sharp breath at his touch, and her eyelashes fluttered almost imperceptibly. "OK."

He barely resisted the urge to do a fist pump. "OK?"

She laughed. "Give me your driver's license before I change my mind."

He handed it over without argument. Then he gave her his best *Zoolander*, model pose when she took his picture, which made her snort laugh. She spent a minute sending texts to her sister and a friend, and then they were on their way.

"I'm not going to get drunk and sleep with you," she warned him as they headed to her place in her lime green Prius.

"I'm not going to get drunk and sleep with *you*, either," he said.

At least, that was the plan...

CHAPTER 5

*I*f she survived this day, she was never, *ever* going to drink another drop of alcohol *ever* again.

Delilah groaned as she turned over, then yelped as she rolled right off the couch onto the floor. Or rather, onto Michael, who was on the floor.

She scrambled off him as gracefully as she could (which wasn't gracefully at all, because her blood alcohol level was probably still three times the normal limit, and she wasn't all that graceful to begin with) and staggered to the window to snap the curtains shut.

The morning light shining into the room felt like the judg-mental finger of God, pointing at her all...judge-y like.

Delilah sat down on the arm of her sofa and lowered her forehead to her palm.

She felt like Slipknot was putting on a concert inside her skull, her entire body ached like she'd done a triathlon, and her mouth tasted like something had crawled into her throat and died there. And not something clean. This taste was like a zombie-fied roadkill skunk had chosen her throat as its final resting place.

Sweet merciful crap, what had they *done* last night?

Tequila shots, she knew immediately, partly because only tequila hangovers made her feel like *this*, and also because she could smell lime juice on her sticky fingers.

Delilah valiantly choked back vomit as she remembered what else she'd consumed along with all that alcohol.

There'd been extra buttery popcorn after the first round of shots while they watched *Attack of the Clones* and mercilessly mocked the dialogue. Then came the Hawaiian pizza and Tai takeout they'd had while mocking *America's Next Top Model* reruns and drinking margaritas.

Somewhere into their binge-watch of *Cobra Kai*, she vaguely remembered trying to do the crane technique, which would explain the pulled muscle she currently felt in her groin area. Michael had attempted it as well, she recalled, and it'd worked beautifully against the ceramic lamp that'd once been on her end table. Now pieces of it were scattered all over the floor between her living room and kitchen.

Then there'd been tequila, several Pop Tarts, a package of Mallomars, tequila, a can of Pringles, tequila…

There was no choking back the vomit this time. She barely made it to the toilet in time to puke up a week's worth of food and a lifetime's worth of tequila.

When she was done—shaky, sweating, and weak, but done—Delilah brushed her teeth and grabbed a hair tie so that when she puked next (and she *would* puke again at some point) she'd at least avoid getting it in her hair.

That's when she made the mistake of glancing up at herself in the mirror.

Holy Mother of *Night of the Living Dead*!

Her skin was three shades whiter than death. Every article of clothing she owned would fit in the bags under her eyes. Her lips were nude—not a hint of pink in them. And her hair...

Medusa herself would look at Delilah's tangled rat's nest and cringe. It took her several tries and a lot of curse words to wrestle it all into the hair tie.

That's when she noticed her outfit for the first time since waking up face-down on her couch.

Or rather, her *lack* of outfit.

She was still wearing her Reylo white tank top, but she'd lost her bra at some point during the night. Her pants were also MIA. She was, however, wearing what looked to be...men's black boxer briefs.

Her mind reeled. Had they...surely they didn't...

Oh, she was going to be *pissed* if she'd had sex with Michael and couldn't remember it.

Chewing on her thumb nail, Delilah tiptoed back into the living room and glanced down at Michael.

He was still sprawled out on her floor, face down, with his head pillowed on one forearm. He was wearing a *whole lot* of nothing.

Shirtless and pant less, the only thing covering any part of his tanned, toned, perfect skin was pink lace panties.

The ones *she'd* been wearing last night.

And his ass looked *amazing* in those panties.

Which was *so* not the point.

With a noise somewhere between a snort and a snore, the sleeping god in pink panties on her floor woke up, rolling to one side. He blinked several times, then squinted up at her, before giving her a lazy, I've-seen-you-naked smile.

"Morning," he murmured sleepily.

Holy hell. He had a giant sleep crease across his forehead,

crazy bedhead, he was wearing women's underwear—and he was still ridiculously fuckable. Meanwhile, she looked like an extra on the set of *The Walking Dead*.

And she couldn't remember whether she'd had sex with him.

Then his gaze dropped to her chest and her nipples immediately rose to the occasion. She crossed her arms over her chest. "So…um…did we…"

He raised that stupid, sexy, smartass brow at her. "Did we have sex? No. Trust me—I'd remember. So would you."

She was simultaneously relieved and disappointed. Relieved that she hadn't had sex with a stranger while in a reckless, drunken state, and bummed that she apparently couldn't even get laid while in a reckless, drunken state.

"Then why are you wearing my underwear?" she asked.

He glanced down at himself, then back up at her. "We both thought it would be hilarious to switch underwear last night." He ran a hand through his hair, then sighed and added, "Now I'm not so sure why we thought that."

"Why aren't you hungover?"

He shrugged. "I don't get hangovers. Never have."

Then he stood up and stretched his arms over his head and she had to look away. Those panties were not containing, um, *all* of him.

And seeing all *that*—along with the rippling muscles—right there in front of her where she could look but not lick, was beyond cruel.

Touch. Look but not *touch.*

"Are you feeling bad?" he asked. "Is there anything I can do?"

Sure. Bend me over the arm of this sofa and bang the hangover right out of me.

Her typical nervous, high-pitched hyena laugh slipped from her lips before she could swallow it back. She'd had it her whole life. It was like a nervous tic she couldn't get rid of. "No. I'll be fine. I just need coffee. And clothes. Yeah, clothes are good."

And with that, she fled the room like the floor was lava and hastily pulled on the first thing she could find, which was a fluffy, oversized gray hoodie and black leggings. When she made it back, she found Michael in her kitchen, firing up the coffee pot. Shirtless. Wearing only yesterday's gray sweatpants.

Sweatpants should *not* be that sexy. But, oh, they were. On him, they were.

And right there on the corner of the sofa, folded up neatly, were the pink panties he'd been wearing a minute ago. Since she was still wearing his boxer briefs under her leggings, under his sweats, he was wearing...

He turned around and her gaze immediately dropped to the front of his sweats. Yep. He was definitely *not* wearing anything under those sweatpants.

And he was a morning person. Or at least, his erection was. It was right there, all hard and huge, pointing at her.

He cleared his throat, and she dragged her guilty gaze back up to his. "You could quit staring at it," he suggested dryly. "That might help it go away."

She choked back another nervous laugh and rubbed her gritty eyes with the heels of her hands. "Sorry."

"No big deal."

Oh, but it was a *big* deal, alright. *Huge.* Ahem.

"Here," he said, gesturing to the barstool at the tiny slab of Formica that separated her kitchen and living room. "Sit." He pressed a steaming cup of black coffee into her hand. "Drink this. It'll help."

She snorted, but did as she was told. "Coffee will help me get over the fact that I made a total ass of myself last night?"

He leaned against the counter and offered her a smile that

would've melted her knees had she been standing. "I made a total ass of myself, too. Maybe we cancelled each other out?"

Delilah took a sip of her coffee, welcoming the stinging, bitter burn against her tongue that let her know the tequila—and subsequent vomit—hadn't fried all her tastebuds. "Other than putting on my panties, I fail to see what *you* did to embarrass yourself."

He narrowed his eyes on her in a way that made her stomach roil again. "What?" she asked. "Why are you looking at me like that?"

"Well...I'm guessing you don't remember anything you texted to anyone last night?"

There was the vomit again, threatening to claw its way up her throat. "What the hell did I do?" she whispered.

The vaguely sympathetic look on his face did absolutely *nothing* to make her feel better. And when he snagged her phone off the stove—why her phone was on the stove, she had *no* fucking idea—and slid it across the counter to her, it took her a solid minute to work up the courage to unlock it and look.

She frowned as she pulled up her texts. "Who is Sadie and why did I text her?"

"Sadie's my ex-fiancée."

Delilah gasped. "No!"

"Yes."

She sputtered. "But...why would you let me do that?"

He ran a hand through his already messy hair and sighed. "I said I don't get hangovers, Delilah, not that I don't get *drunk*. You thought it would be hilarious to text Sadie, and I was drunk enough to give you the number."

"She texted me back," she murmured. "She said, 'Can't wait to see you on Saturday. I've added you to the guest list as Michael's plus one.'"

She lifted her eyes to his, and Michael winced. "Yeah. If you scroll back, I think you'll see that you told her we were dating, that I was the 'most awesomest boyfriend ev-ah' and that you'd love to go to the wedding with me."

Delilah slapped a palm over her mouth in horror. She *had* texted that! Her mother—a third grade English teacher— would be appalled by her mangled grammar. Then she dropped her forehead to the counter when she realized she'd also sent an accompanying image.

"Oh, God," she groaned and thrust her phone at him. "I can't look. Just tell me…what picture did I send her? Please tell me I wasn't mooning her or something."

"No," he said immediately. "That picture wasn't embarrassing at all." He shoved her phone toward her again. "See? It's just a selfie of the two of us."

She cracked one eye open first, then the other. He was right. It wasn't embarrassing. It was a decent picture. They had their faces squished together and ear-to-ear grins in place. It had been taken before her makeup melted off, so her face wasn't a total wreck.

And shock of all shocks: Michael was incredibly photo-genic and luscious looking, even when drunk off his ass. Bastard.

Then a thought occurred to her. A scary, horrible thought…

She swallowed hard and looked him dead in the eye. "You said '*that* picture wasn't embarrassing.' What other pictures are out there?"

He rubbed a hand over the back of his neck and averted his eyes. "You sent some messages to Steve," he mumbled.

With shaking fingers, she started scrolling, half expecting to see weepy, drunk "why didn't you love me more" messages. What she found instead was…interesting.

"Um..." she held the phone up so that Michael could see the photo she'd sent to Steve. "Is this your..."

"Yes," he confirmed, much to her chagrin. "That is indeed my penis."

"And that's my face right there next to it, huh?"

"Well, yeah, see, you were holding the ruler."

"Obviously," she muttered. The text she sent along with the photo of her face within licking distance of Michael's dick said, "FINALLY I don't have to fake orgasms anymore. FINALLY someone other than me can reach my G-spot."

Holy. Shitballs.

And since that time, Steve had sent no fewer than ten replies. The last one just said, "We need to talk."

Yeah, like *that* was going to happen. She'd be too busy procuring a new identity and planning her move to Yemin to talk to Steve ever again.

"I'm really sorry," Michael said. "It seemed like such a funny idea at the time. I'll send out apologies to Steve and Sadie. You can throw me under the bus and say I stole your phone and sent the messages myself. Whatever you want."

He sounded so sincere. He really *would* let her throw him under the bus. Other than when he'd come to her rescue yesterday, it was the nicest thing anyone had offered to do for her in a very long time. It would've warmed her heart if she wasn't so painfully hungover.

She sighed. "It's OK. I mean, it's not like I care what Steve thinks anymore. And I didn't send anything lethally embarrassing to Sadie, so I should be able to show my face at the wedding without wanting to die."

He blinked at her. "You mean you'd really consider going with me?"

She blinked back at him. "Don't you want me to?"

"Of course, I do! I just thought after all this…"

The quickness with which he'd said he wanted her to be his date at the wedding did great things for her ego. "Hey, after what you did for me at the grocery yesterday, I think being your wedding date and fake girlfriend is the *least* I can do."

He grinned at her. "You could *definitely* do less. I got the better end of this deal, trust me. I'll still owe you one."

She glanced back down at the photo on her phone.

It was hard to tell because her contacts weren't in, but…did that ruler say ten inches?

Wow. Just…*wow*.

She wished she was still drunk so that she could insist he owed her *ten*, not one. Inches, that is. Ten hot, hard inches.

But that'd never happen, because she was never, ever, *ever* drinking again.

That's my story and I'm sticking to it.

CHAPTER 6

*A*fter Michael called an Uber and headed back to the grocery to get his car, Delilah scrolled through her phone to see what other disasters she might have created for herself last night, and realized she'd missed no less than eight texts and a handful of calls from her sister, Val.

If Delilah could kick herself, she would've. *Of course,* her sister was concerned. She'd texted her some strange guy's picture along with the words "If I end up dead, it was this guy who killed me."

Geez, she really had *not* been at her best last night.

Val picked up on the first ring and didn't wait for Delilah's greeting before she said, "I was just putting the kids' shoes on so that we could come to your apartment and make sure you aren't dead."

Delilah sighed. "I'm sorry, Val. I'm kinda surprised you didn't show up last night, frankly."

There was a pause on Val's end, and Delilah heard one of the kids ask about breakfast.

Val told the child—whichever one it was—that she'd make pancakes as soon as she was off the phone, then told Delilah, "Ben convinced me that you were probably getting laid, not murdered, and I didn't want to screw that up for you."

Delilah supposed she owed her brother-in-law a beer. The last thing she'd needed last night was her overprotective big sister showing up and letting Michael know just how deep in her family the crazy ran.

And it ran *deep*. Like the mighty Mississippi.

She side-stepped the issue of whether or not she might've gotten laid last night by asking, "Was that Brady asking about breakfast? Tell him 'hi' from Auntie Delilah."

"That was Brandon," she said, sounding exhausted. "But I'll tell them both you said 'hi'. Maddie, too."

Val's three kids were all under the age of six. Brady and Brandon were twin four-year-olds. Their big sister Maddie was five.

See? Banana-pants crazy.

But Val had always been crazy in a good, productive way, while Delilah's crazy leaned more toward the chaotic and destructive.

Val was every parent's wet dream. While Delilah was smoking pot under the bleachers in high school with the other band geeks, Val was studying and getting straight A's. When Delilah was barely scraping by in college with C's, Val was making the LSATs her bitch and getting into law school.

When Delilah was dating a commitment-phobic loser who would one day cheat on her, Val was marrying Ben, the perfect man, who just so happened to be a hot pediatric surgeon. And while Delilah's eggs were drying up (as her mother liked to tell her every Sunday at family dinner), Val was fertile as potting soil.

And just for funsies, Val was also three inches taller, ten pounds lighter, and had a thick, wavy head of natural blonde hair that would make angels weep with jealousy.

If she didn't love her so much, Delilah would hate her on principle.

"I'm so sorry I worried you," Delilah said. "Everything's fine, though."

Val snorted. "I guess you *would* say everything is *fine*. That was maybe the most attractive man I've ever seen."

In the background, she heard Ben mumble a protest, to which Val said, "Oh, shut up. You're the father of my children. *Of course,* I think you're attractive. This guy is just more attractive in an obvious, conventional way. Don't get all insecure."

Delilah couldn't hold back a grin. Ben could protest and act disgruntled all he wanted, but he was the happiest married man Delilah had ever seen in her life. He was one half of the ultimate power couple, and there was no way he was ever going to be threatened by a little thing like his wife finding another man attractive.

Delilah had once heard Ben and Val discussing, very earnestly, their "freebie" lists—the list of celebrities they were allowed to fuck if they ever got the opportunity—without fear of repercussions. Ben had told Val that he'd divorce her if she was foolish enough not to "ride that ride" if she ever got a shot at Jason Momoa.

"He's very attractive, yes," Delilah said. "But nothing happened." Well, nothing other than general drunken asshattery, that is. "I am going out with him again, though."

Ten minutes later, Delilah had filled Val in on the whole crazy story, from their supermarket meet cute (not), to their drunken underwear swap, to the penis measuring.

She forwarded the accompanying photos, too. They were too amazing to keep to herself.

By the end, Val was laughing so hard she sounded like she was struggling to catch her breath, which made Delilah smile. At least her humiliation could provide this much-needed humor to her sister's life.

"Oh, God," Val said between chuckles. "I wish I could've seen that bastard Steve's face when he opened that text."

Val had always hated Steve. Even back when they'd just started dating, back when he was still a good guy and not the complete turd he became, Val had told Delilah that Steve wasn't good enough for her. She'd always just assumed her sister was holding Steve to the impossibly high bar Ben had set. But, alas, no. She'd just been right.

"He texted that we needed to talk," Delilah admitted.

That ended Val's laughter abruptly. "I hope you told him to piss off."

She sighed. "I didn't tell him anything. But, I mean, I don't see what he could possibly have to say to me anymore."

"Excuses. Lies. Anything designed to keep you pining for him while he continues to play with his little fuck toy," Val said dispassionately.

Then, in the background, Delilah very clearly heard Brady— or was it Brandon?—repeat, "fuck toy" in his sweet little voice, and she wasn't *at all* ashamed to admit it made her day.

After explaining to Brady (or maybe Brandon) why he shouldn't repeat any of the words mommy ever said to Auntie Delilah, Val let out a deep breath and said, "Well, you just know *that's* going to come back to haunt me on the first day of kindergarten. Or worse, at church."

"Meh, don't worry about it," Delilah said. "Mom will blame me, not you, no matter what."

Val sniffed. "Good point. But anyhoo, what's going on with Mr. 10-inches? You said you're going out again? He'd make a *great* rebound."

Delilah snorted. If she knew her sister, Val had pulled out her readers to clearly see the numbers on the ruler in the photo. And she wasn't even going to address the ridiculousness of using someone like Michael as a rebound. What a waste of a hot, hilarious nerd man *that* would be.

No, the best they could probably hope for was to end up friends, since she had no intention of doing the relationship thing again any time soon.

"Well, since I made a damn fool of myself and texted his ex, begging for an invite to her wedding, I've graciously agreed to be Michael's date this weekend."

He'd probably gotten the short end of the stick in that deal, now that she thought about it. She didn't traditionally do well with parents. Her tendency to blurt out embarrassing crap when she was nervous (and the fact that parents made her nervous) meant she wasn't the girl- you-can-take-home-to-mom kind. She supposed she was more of a girl-you-date-in-secret-and-pretend-you're-just-friends- with-around-every-one-else type.

Steve's parents, who only ever referred to her as "that girl" (usually said with a pinched expression like they'd just sniffed a fresh pile of dog crap) or Darcy (because Delilah was just too complicated to remember, apparently) could certainly attest to that.

After a long pause, Val asked, "You're going with him to a *wedding?*"

"Yeah. It's no big deal. He needed a date. He helped me out with Steve, so why not?"

Val sputtered for a second or two. "Because a *wedding* is a *serious* date, not a rebound, getting-back-in-the-saddle kind of date."

Well, that struck Delilah mute for a moment. But only for a moment. "Are *you*—the woman who has been in league with mom for the past *decade* to see me married with children as quickly as humanly possible—*seriously* telling me you want me to go on some kind of pathetic *rebound* date, like bowling or some shit, with a loser I have no interest in long term, rather than go with Michael to his ex's wedding? Because the irony of *that* is just comical as hell."

Val sighed and said, "I just want you to go out. Have fun. Date around a little. You haven't had time to do that. You're still young, but Steve took up *way* too many of your good, viable dating years. I don't want to see you fall for the next decent guy you meet and end up hurt again. I mean, is Mr. 10-inches *really* looking for a girlfriend—or is he just using you for a wedding date?"

Well, *that* made her sound like a big old lame-ass loser, didn't it? Poor little Delilah…not much dating history to speak of, setting herself up to fall for the hot guy who only wants to use her as a tool to get through his ex's wedding.

"I don't know what Michael is looking for, Val," she said very carefully, "because we only just met. It's one wedding date. I'm not expecting him to propose at the end of the evening, OK? I may not have an extensive dating history, but I'm not *that* naïve."

"I never said you were naïve," Val said defensively. "I'm just saying…oh, hell, Delilah, I just don't want to see you hurt, and Mr. 10 Inches looks like heartbreak walking. That's all. I'm sorry if I offended you."

Offended wasn't the right word, she supposed. Insulted? Maybe a little. But not intentionally. She knew Val always had her big sister hat on, and it was probably hard for someone as perfect as her to watch Delilah stumble through life with messed-up hair, mismatched socks, and a romantic history that could only be described as tragic.

"It's OK," Delilah eventually said. "I know you mean well. But you don't have to worry. I'm not looking for another relationship. Not anytime soon, at least. I'm not looking for a rebound, either. I'm going to this wedding with Michael as a favor to a new *friend* who did me a solid with Steve and Sherry last night. That's all."

"Well, you better make sure he knows that," Val grumbled. "Because a wedding date comes with expectations. He might want more than you're ready to give."

She frowned. There was no way Michael had *those* kinds of expectations going into the date.

They were *friends*. They would *remain* friends.

And that's all there was to it.

CHAPTER 7

*M*ichael sat down in the teacher's lounge with a groan, idly wondering when he'd started turning into his dad. Now *there* was a man who'd never taken a seat without sounding like he'd been on his feet for *years*.

But teaching art to privileged 3rd graders who had *zero* interest in it was *not* for the faint of heart, so he decided to cut himself some slack.

That's when he pulled out his phone and noticed a text from Delilah. He smiled. Maybe his day was looking up after all.

Delilah: *I want to make sure that I didn't give you the wrong impression when I agreed to go to the wedding with you. We should probably set some ground rules.*

His smile slipped. OK, *this* was much more in line with how his day was going. In his experience, no good (or fun) *ever* came from setting ground rules.

Michael: *Are we talking simple guidelines for behavior, or something a little more elaborate...like the Sokovia Accords?*

He didn't have to wait long for the three little dots to pop up, indicating that she was responding. Seemed that Delilah typed as fast as she talked.

Delilah: *Well, I don't think we need to involve the UN or the Avengers...but probably more like the Sokovia Accords?*

Michael: *So, this text is a summit to establish the accords?*

Delilah: *OMG, you really ARE a huge nerd!*

Michael: *I tried to tell you...*

Then he attached a GIF of Steve Urkel snapping his suspenders that he was *sure* would make her snort laugh. He'd discovered that few things in the world were more adorable than Delilah snort laughing.

Delilah: *Ugh. You just made me laugh until I snorted! Damn you!*

Michael did a mental fist pump. Mission accomplished!

Michael: *Well, you called this summit, so, I'll leave it up to you name it.*

Delilah: *How about the We're Just Friends Because I'm Rebounding Off a Bad Relationship And Not Ready for Anything More Serious Accords?*

He groaned like an old man again. Yeah, he figured that was where this was going. She was afraid all the drunken semi-nudity they'd shared had given him the wrong idea about the nature of their upcoming wedding date. He'd just been stiff-armed into the friendzone.

Awesome.

The only thing that could make this day worse would be catching the stomach bug that'd made Stanley Frakes crap his pants in fourth period.

Michael: *Well, it's kinda long and doesn't have much of a ring to it. How about we just call it the We're Just Friends Accords, established at the Friendzone Summit?*

Delilah: *And that's OK with you?*

Michael thought about his answer for a moment. Was it OK

with him? Of course, it was. If a woman didn't want to date him, that was her prerogative. Was he disappointed?

Fuck, yes.

Delilah was the most desirable woman he'd met in a long time, and she'd just told him she didn't want him. It was a kick to the nuts, to be sure.

But he liked her enough to take whatever she was willing to give—and if that was only friendship, so be it.

Michael: *Of course, it's OK. You're in charge. Besides, you just met me. I wasn't expecting you to propose or anything.*

He attached a GIF of Klinger from MASH in a wedding dress to emphasize his point...and to earn another snort laugh.

Her reply came in the form of ten laughing emojis.

They exchanged a few more texts after that working out the details. Yes, they could drive home after the rehearsal dinner and back to the resort again the next day for the ceremony, as opposed to staying there. It was only an hour away.

Not that he wouldn't have been *more* than willing to spend the entire weekend in a hotel room with her—clothing optional, of course.

But friends didn't imagine friends naked and bent over a hotel dresser, so he needed to stop that train of thought before it left the station.

Too late.

When all the details were finalized, he was surprised to see another text come through.

Delilah: *I should probably warn you...parents make me nervous. And when I'm nervous, I babble. It can get embarrassing.*

Michael didn't really see a problem with that. When he'd introduced Katie to his parents, she'd spent the night puking in the guest bathroom. Nervous stomach, she'd said. He didn't imagine Delilah's nervous babbling could be any worse than that.

Michael: *You don't have anything to be nervous about around my family. They're all crazy. A little bit of babble won't even phase them. But, if it makes you feel better, we can have a code word. When you get nervous and need me to bail you out or something, just use the code word.*

Delilah: *A code word? Like people use when they're having rough sex or something?*

Wow, I really wish you wouldn't have said that.

Because now, Michael was thinking about Delilah naked and bent over the hotel dresser with her hands tied behind her back.

Nothing like texting with a woman who'd just friendzoned you while sporting a raging hard on. He had to delete his next eight potential replies because they were completely overloaded with innuendo. Totally not appropriate for the Friendzone Summit or the We're Just Friends Accords.

Michael: *Let the record reflect that one Delilah Morgenstern brought sex into the official accords.*

Delilah: *I object! You're the one talking about safe words!*

Michael: Code *words,* NOT *safe words.*

Delilah: *Oh. Well...awkward!*

Michael: *No worries. The code word should be something that doesn't come up in normal conversation.*

Delilah: *I dunno. I use A LOT of words in normal conversation.*

Michael: *I knew that about you. It can be something completely off the wall if you want.*

Delilah: *How about bumfuzzle?*

Michael: *You made that up, didn't you?*

Delilah: *No! It's something my grandma used to say. It means being confused or flustered.*

Michael: *OK. Bumfuzzle it is. So, if you're nervous and feel like you need an assist, just say bumfuzzle and I'll help you out.*

Delilah: *Thanks for understanding, Michael. You really are a nice guy.*

Michael winced. Great. He was nice guy, which loosely translated to Guy Who Never, Ever, EVER gets the girl.

Another old man groan. And the hits just kept on coming.

The way his day was going, he expected that stomach bug to strike any minute now.

CHAPTER 8

"*Y*ou are absolutely *wrong*."

Michael kept his eyes on the road, but could see Delilah in his peripheral vision, shaking her head at him.

They'd been driving for about thirty minutes, had another thirty or so to go—maybe more, if the heavy, wet snow that was starting to come down at an alarming rate started sticking to the roads—and still, he wasn't anxious to get out of the car. He had Delilah to thank for that.

Verbally sparring with her was the most fun he'd had in, well, *ever* maybe.

When she was particularly passionate about a topic, her cheeks flushed pink, her eyes sparkled, and she started talking with her hands.

She'd accidentally smacked him in the shoulder twice while they were discussing the direction Disney was taking the Star Wars franchise (which was right into the misogynistic toilet, except for *The Mandalorian*, of course), why DC comics were so great and the films were so dreadful, and why they both secretly wished it'd been Captain America who'd died in *Avengers Endgame* instead of Tony Stark.

She was *especially* animated right now, and he almost wished he could pull the car over so he could watch her instead of the road.

If she got this excited talking about television and movies, what would she look like pinned under him, with all that wild auburn hair spread out across his bedsheets, while he made her come until she lost her voice from screaming his name so long and so loud?

"And *that's* why *Diehard* is abso-*fuckin'*-lutely a Christmas movie."

And that's also when Michael realized he'd been too busy fantasizing about fucking her to listen to what she'd been saying.

It was 100% a violation of the We're Just Friends Accords they'd reached at the Friendzone Summit. He should be ashamed of himself.

But he wasn't. Not really. He couldn't help it. He was a guy, she was hot, and he liked her. A *lot*.

Accords could be always be amended if all parties involved were agreeable to the changes…right?

He cleared his throat. "Look, all I said was *Diehard* isn't a Christmas movie and that a movie should have to have more than a *mention* of the holidays in it to be considered a Christmas movie. I still maintain that's true."

"And I just explained why you're wrong. Now all you can do is sit there in your wrongness and live with how wrong you are."

He chuckled. "OK, fair enough."

She grinned at him and thrust her bag of road food toward him. "Twizzlers?"

"No thanks. I'm more of a Red Vines guy."

Delilah blew a raspberry at him like an agitated chimp. "Red Vines. You mean Twizzlers' ugly second cousin? No thanks. But at least you're not anti-sugar. Steve *hated* to travel anywhere with me because of my road food. He said he was going to get diabetes just by being too close to it."

Michael felt his lip curl involuntarily at the mention of Delilah's ex. What kind of stuck-up tool traveled without candy? And more importantly, what kind of cuntmuffin wouldn't gladly buy a woman like Delilah as much fucking candy as she wanted if it made her happy?

"Why were you with a fuckwit like that, anyway?" Michael asked before he'd had a chance to think better of it.

She was quiet for a moment, and he worried that he'd offended her. He *had* just blurted out what was a fairly rude question, after all.

But after a long pause, she let out a deep sigh and said, "He wasn't always a fuckwit. When we first started dating, he was a sweet, shy, nerdy guy. He treated me like a queen. We were best friends."

Another pause. Michael glanced over at her and the sad, wistful smile on her face made his heart ache. He knew better than anyone what it was like to lose your best friend when the romantic relationship fell to shit.

"It wasn't until he graduated and started working toward partner at his accounting firm that he started changing," she said. "One night, one of the senior partners told him he'd never make partner if he didn't start caring more about appearances and learning to schmooze the clients. Steve was obsessed after that. He lost weight, bought all new clothes, got cultured and started hounding me to do the same."

"He's an idiot," Michael grumbled.

She shrugged in a gesture that she probably hoped looked careless, but Michael could see it wasn't. She was still hurt by what that asshole did to her.

Instead of pretending to be her boyfriend, Michael should've broken the fucker's nose when he'd had the chance.

"Thanks," she said quietly. "Honestly though, I was the idiot. I should've left him long before he left me. I guess I was just still hung up on what we had in the past. I still miss his friendship. The friendship I had with the *old* Steve, you know?"

He reached over and grabbed her hand, giving her fingers a firm squeeze. "You're not an idiot. You were hopeful that someone you loved would come to his senses and realize how good he had it. That's not stupid, it's…romantic. One of these days, he's going to realize that he gave up the best thing he ever had in exchange for a job title."

She chuckled without a hint of actual humor. "And the new Barbie doll girlfriend. Don't forget about her."

"She's *nothing* compared to you."

Michael blinked at the unexpected fervor of his words. Christ, he'd really said that with his *whole* chest. He probably sounded like an obsessed stalker.

He didn't glance over at her, but he could feel her unblinking attention on him. He cleared his throat. "I think I'll take a Twizzler after all," he mumbled.

She let go of his hand, then pressed a Twizzler into it.

Maybe if his mouth was full, he'd quit saying stupid, embarrassing shit to a woman who'd made it clear she didn't want more than friendship from him at the moment.

It was a long shot, but what other options did he have?

~

By the time Michael pulled into the resort parking lot, Delilah's bladder was about to explode, her left butt cheek was completely numb, and there were at least three inches of snow covering the roads.

The weather reports Michael was listening to were grim as fuck, too. She'd be shocked if everyone who was supposed to come tonight actually made it. In fact, they could get stranded here, too, which is why Delilah always carried a go-bag that included her camera, a toothbrush, and a change of clothes anytime she traveled somewhere more than twenty miles from her house.

And since this event was formal, her go-bag also included make-up and hair care products.

Michael had chuckled when he loaded her go-bag into the trunk and teased her about it, but tonight, when they were stuck here and he had nothing but the clothes on his back and a suit in a garment bag, he'd be jealous of her freshly brushed teeth and clean underwear.

Her own formal dress was also in a garment bag in the trunk. She'd agonized over which dress she should bring. Her little black dress was stylish, elegant, and not too revealing. It definitely said "classy wedding with a friend."

Her little *red* dress, on the other hand…

Well, *that* dress said, "we're gonna bang when we leave here. Hard."

The black dress was clearly the responsible choice.

Which was why she'd packed the red dress.

Responsible had never really been her thing.

Delilah couldn't help herself. No matter how hard she'd shoved Michael into the friendzone, she still wanted him to think she was pretty. Sexy. Highly fuckable.

But she refused to analyze it too much. She was fresh out of a long-term relationship where she'd been hurt. It was only natural that she'd want the attention of a nice, smart, stupidly sexy man.

It *certainly* wasn't that she was rebounding into something serious, because that'd just be proving her sister right, and Delilah wasn't about to let *that* happen.

Michael cursed as the rear end of his SUV fishtailed in the snow, but he quickly got it under control and managed to skid into a parking space near the resort's entrance.

She shot him a pointed look. "My go-bag isn't so funny now, is it?"

He side-eyed her and gave her a crooked grin. "It was never that funny. I brought one, too." He shrugged. "You just never know."

Delilah sputtered. "You teased me for bringing that bag! Called me Paranoid Polly."

Another shrug. "You're fun to tease. You get all fired up and the blush goes all the way down your neck. It's sexy."

He grinned at her, totally innocent, as if calling her sexy wasn't the verbal equivalent of him reaching over and sliding his hand into her panties. All she could do was sit there, slack-jawed, and completely turned on.

"Stay there," he told her. "I'll grab the bags, then I'll come around and help you out. This parking lot hasn't been treated and I don't want you to fall."

And with that, he pulled the hood of his gray sweatshirt up and slid out to grab the bags.

He was gentlemanly. Protective. Thought her ex was a douchebag tool and wasn't afraid to say so out loud. He had an uncommon degree of nerd knowledge. He was the most beautiful man she'd ever seen in real life. He thought *she* was sexy.

And she was supposed to *not* rebound with him or fall for him?

She couldn't hold in a snort of derision.

Yeah. Sure. What could possibly go wrong?

CHAPTER 9

*T*he resort Sadie had chosen for her rehearsal dinner and ceremony was perfect. It was upscale, but not so upscale that it was unaffordable or intimidating.

The lobby had a high-end cabin feel to it, with sitting areas filled with overstuffed leather loveseats and chairs, and natural pine end and coffee tables. The lighting was soft and natural, and floor-to-ceiling windows provided a lovely view of the snow piling up outside.

A huge stone fireplace held a roaring fire that crackled pleasantly in accompaniment to the gentle classical music that was playing overhead. Beyond the fireplace was a reception desk that appeared to be made of planks of cedar, polished and shellacked to a high shine.

The place also boasted a quaint, cozy chapel and a reception hall that could be customized to fit anything from a small, family affair to a royal one.

Overall, the resort was elegant, refined, beautiful, but not at all pretentious or stuffy. Exactly like the bride-to-be, Michael mused.

Next to him (well, tucked up against his side, actually) Delilah made a grab for her bag, which he neatly held up out of her reach.

She pursed her lips and shot him a squinty-eyed, annoyed look that shouldn't have done anything to arouse his libido.

But it did.

"We're inside now," she said on an exasperated huff. "No chance of me falling on my ass in the snow. I can walk on my own and carry my own bag. I'm not a child."

Didn't he fucking know it.

Reluctantly, he shifted his arm off her shoulders and let her move away from him, but there was no way in hell he was handing the bag over. The thing probably weighed more than she did, and even though he wasn't much of a gentleman, he knew better than to let a lady carry her own luggage.

"If you want to go stand by the fire and warm up, I'll check at the front desk and see if there's a place we can change clothes and stow your serial killer go-bag while we're at dinner," he said.

There went the blush. It started in her cheeks and very quickly went down her neck, under her rainbow-colored knitted scarf, and into the *Doctor Who* T-shirt she was currently rocking the *hell* out of. In that moment, he'd give *anything* to be able to follow that blush with his fingertips. Or his tongue. Or his...

"I told you, it's just my camera, a change of clothes, and some makeup," she said. "Nothing serial killer-y about it. And *you* admitted to having a go-bag, too. So, since 92.5% of serial killers are male, and a huge majority of those are *white* males, it's much more likely that *you're* Hannibal Lector in this scenario, not me."

He chuckled. "Well, while your knowledge of serial killer statistics is undeniably hot, and while I *certainly* wouldn't mind taking a bite out of you, I am not Hannibal Lector. You're safe with me, Delilah."

She sucked in a sharp breath and he fought the urge to let his gaze drop to check out how her breasts rose and fell with the action. "Ok, I'm going to need you to stop doing *that*," she said, waving a finger to gesture at, well, all of him.

"What?"

"The whole *charming* thing. Being *that* nice and flirty in combination with *that* face and *that* body is just, well, it's sensory overload, you know? If we're going to do the just friends thing, I can't handle all *that*. You're going to need to take it down a notch."

And the takeaway he got out of all *that*, was that she wanted him, too. *Oh, thank you, Jesus.*

He took a step into her personal space and brushed his fingertips over the smooth slope of her cheekbone. "I'd rather not," he murmured. "See, I'm thinking I'd like to renegotiate the We're Just Friends Accords."

She sputtered, but he noticed she didn't take a step back to put distance between them, and she didn't pull away from his touch. If anything, she leaned into his hand ever so slightly. "You can't just renegotiate accords like that," she whispered breathlessly.

"We're not the UN, Delilah. Of *course*, we can renegotiate. I like you. A lot. And I won't do anything to make you uncomfortable. If you're not ready to date yet, that's fine. I'll wait for you."

He leaned down a little so that they were eye to eye and

added, "But I can't pretend that I'm not wildly attracted to you. We've been honest with each other from the start. I don't see why we'd change that now."

She visibly gulped. "Michael, I'm—"

And that's when someone grabbed him from behind, spun him around, and squeezed him so hard he thought his ribs might crack.

"About damn time you got here," his attacker said.

Michael wheezed out a chuckle and wrapped his arms around his big sister to return her hug. For a woman who was eight inches shorter and fifty pounds lighter than him, Grace was freakishly strong.

When she pulled out of his arms to smile up at him, Michael couldn't help but grin back. Happiness sure looked good on her. "Where's my favorite niece?"

She raised a blonde brow at him. "You mean your *only* niece? She's with my neighbor. You remember, you met her last year?"

"The realtor?"

"Yes, that's her. She just got married—you met him, too. He's a chiropractor—and they're thinking about adopting a baby, so they asked to watch Ellis this weekend as practice. They'll do great. Ellis adores them both. And meanwhile, now that I'm childless for a whole weekend, *I* will be getting drunk and taking advantage of my hot husband whenever I get the chance."

Michael winced. "Not something I needed to know."

She shrugged. "Bygones." Then she shifted her shrewd, lawyer-ly gaze to Delilah, who still looked shell-shocked by what he'd told her before Grace so rudely interrupted them.

Grace held her hand out to Delilah. "Hi. I'm Grace, this idiot's big sister."

Delilah shook her hand and let out a nervous chuckle. "I'm Delilah. And I'm probably going to say lots of stupid stuff because meeting new people makes me edgy. I've never been good with meeting my boyfriends' family." She shifted her gaze to Michael. "I'm dangerously close to bumfuzzle territory, here."

Michael slid his hand under her hair and cupped the back of her neck as he smiled down at her. "Talk as much or as little as you want. *Say* whatever you want. I'm just glad you're here with me."

Grace's gaze bopped between them like she was watching a tennis match before a slow smile overtook her. "Delilah, I'm *so* happy to meet you. I can't even tell you how much."

Michael narrowed his eyes on his sister. Was it just his imagination, or was his sister's smile decidedly smug?

CHAPTER 10

*a*s it turned out, Sadie was a smart lady who liked to plan for the worst, because she'd had the foresight to book several extra rooms, just in case anyone who'd planned to leave after the rehearsal dinner got stuck there.

And according to the recent weather reports (and the metric fuckton of snow that was currently blanketing their half of the state), *everyone* who'd made it to the rehearsal dinner was going to want to stay there tonight.

Several out-of-state guests who were supposed to fly in tonight for the wedding tomorrow had already called to say they wouldn't be able to make it, too, which Grace said Sadie was handling with the kind of serene calm that was just unnatural for a bride on the eve of her wedding.

But since everything had gone wrong at Sadie's *last* wedding (including the fact that she fell in love with the groom's cousin), Delilah imagined a little snow was nothing to get too worked up about.

The good news was that Delilah and Michael had a room

waiting for them, so they wouldn't have to get ready for dinner in a resort bathroom as they'd assumed they would. The bad news?

They had *one* room. With *one* King-sized bed. To share.

As soon as the desk clerk handed them an electronic keycard to the room Sadie had reserved for them, Michael had given Delilah a questioning look. He was willing to find another place to stay if she was uncomfortable sharing a room with him. She could see it in his eyes.

But making him stay elsewhere just seemed silly. They had already spent one night together, drinking to the point of near alcohol poisoning. Swapping underwear. Measuring erections. Was there really any reason to get all modest now, when they were both sober and pretending to be boyfriend and girlfriend?

Delilah couldn't think of a good reason to object to the room arrangements, so she didn't. She'd shrugged it off and followed Michael up to their lavishly appointed room.

With the one King-sized bed they would be sharing tonight.

Delilah's brain kept drifting back to that one bed as she changed clothes, put on some make-up, and tried to tame her hair into some semblance of normal for the rehearsal dinner.

This was going to be a long night. Not only did she have to pretend to be normal with a group of strangers and not a complete loser with a tendency to blurt out inappropriate comments, but she also had to get through an entire formal dinner knowing that she was coming back to this room to sleep in one bed with a guy who'd admitted he was attracted to her. A guy *she* was attracted to.

A guy she wasn't sure she was ready to date just yet.

She didn't want Michael to be a rebound, damn it. She wanted more, but their timing was *all* wrong. He was probably overly emotional about being at this wedding, watching his first love marry his cousin, and she was fresh off getting dumped by *her* first love. How could anything *real* happen between them now when everything was so messy?

Glancing down at her dress, she realized she should've packed the elegant black dress instead of the fuck-me red one. There was nothing about her current outfit that said "just friends."

Oh well, at least she wouldn't feel frumpy next to Michael's impossibly gorgeous sister. If there was a bright side to all this, she imagined that was it.

Not that Grace was intimidating or anything. If anything, she'd gone out of her way to make Delilah feel comfortable. She'd even acted like Delilah's verbal diarrhea wasn't weird in any way.

Hopefully the rest of Michael's family would be similarly welcoming.

Maybe they'd all be too hyped up from the rehearsal to even pay any attention to her. She could hope, anyway.

She'd been surprised when Michael opted out of the rehearsal, though. She figured his presence would be required. But he'd begged off, claiming he had to make some calls to make sure everything was in order for some field trip his class was taking the following week.

Delilah knew it was a bullshit excuse. He'd had a visible knot of tension in his shoulders since Grace grabbed him and bear-hugged him in the lobby.

Even if he wasn't in love with Sadie anymore, he clearly wasn't unaffected by the thought of watching her commit to someone else—his cousin, no less—for the rest of her life.

Delilah let him get away with it, too. It wasn't her place to get him to open up and discuss his feelings. It's not like she was his *real* girlfriend.

Keep reminding yourself of that, girl. You're gonna need to keep that in mind all *weekend...and especially tonight in that bed...*

~

When Delilah stepped out of the bathroom, Michael forgot why they were there. He forgot all about family, weddings, and pretty much everything else. Hell, he forgot his own name.

She looked *that* amazing.

Delilah was always beautiful. Whether she was makeup-less, wearing a T-shirt and sweats, or first thing in the morning, nursing a hangover, she was a stunner. But right now? She was *otherworldly* beautiful.

Her red dress was made of some kind of slippery material that flowed over the curves of her body and moved with her in a way that suggested it'd been tailored perfectly to drive him out of his fucking mind.

The front draped low enough to make things interesting (very, *very* interesting if his instant erection was any indication), but not low enough to look trashy or like she was trying too hard to get attention. The skirt flirted with her knees, but there was a slit on one side that showed an impressive amount of toned thigh.

Her shoes—strappy, four-inch stilettos that perfectly matched the dress—all but *screamed* fuck me. In that moment, Michael would've given *anything* to feel those heels digging into his back as she wrapped her legs around his waist and he sank into her.

It took a minute to get over the shock of the dress and the heels, but he finally managed to shift his attention from her body to her face. It was no less stunning than the rest of her.

Her makeup was light but seemed to be expertly applied to

highlight her assets (of which she had *many*). And her hair was down, trailing past her shoulders in loose curls.

She bit down on her lower lip—which was shiny with a dark red gloss he'd *kill* to see smeared all over his skin as she trailed her lips down his body—as her gaze met his.

"Is it too much?" she asked, shifting her weight from one foot to the other.

Too much for me to survive? Probably.

He had to swallow hard a couple of times and clear his throat, but he finally managed to find his voice. "You're gorgeous."

She took a deep breath, and he forced himself to maintain eye contact and not let his gaze drop down to watch the rise of and fall of her breasts.

Then she gave him a slow, shy smile and said, "You're pretty gorgeous yourself. You clean-up nice, Poindexter."

She looked so far out of his league right now it'd take the *light* of her league a million years to shine on him. But if she thought he looked good in a suit, he guessed that's all that mattered.

He stepped forward and offered her his arm. "Shall we?"

Delilah slipped her arm through his and grinned up at him. "Let's."

"Are you sure you're ready for this?"

"No," she said immediately. "But how bad can it be?"

He groaned. "Oh, I *really* wish you hadn't said that, sweetheart."

CHAPTER 11

The small, intimate, private room the wedding party reserved for the rehearsal dinner was nothing short of stunning. Exotic-looking arrangements of flowers Delilah wasn't sophisticated enough to name were everywhere, and there were so many candles on the cream-colored, linen-draped tables that she vaguely wondered if it was a fire hazard.

And on Michael's arm, she felt like a princess heading into a grand ball. Or maybe prom queen? Either way, she felt damn elegant, which was a first for her.

Grace, who was the only other person in the room so far, stopped fussing with one of the flower arrangements long enough to give Delilah a hug.

Michael raised a brow at his sister, who seemed a little unsteady on her feet. "Had some wine, sis?"

She blew a raspberry at him. "Don't be judge-y. I told you I was drinking and having lots of sex this weekend."

He winced. "And I told you I didn't want to hear about your sex life."

Grace grabbed Delilah's arm and turned her toward the door in time to see a tall, insanely attractive guy headed in their direction, giving Grace a smile with enough heat behind it to melt all the candle wax in the room. "I have a *great* sex life," she confided in a ridiculously loud stage whisper. "*That's* my husband, Nick."

"Holy fucking Wolverine!" Delilah blurted.

Grace cackled, swayed a little on her heels, and said, "Right?"

Grace knuckle-bumped her, and Delilah grinned. It was *hilarious* to see a prim-looking lawyer in an elegant black dress, drunken knuckle-bumping a near stranger. "You go, girl."

"Oh, come on," Michael said, sounding disgruntled. "He's not *that* good looking."

"Yes, he is," Delilah and Grace said in stereo.

He was, too. Michael was hot in a boy next door, perfect bone structure and lean muscles kind of way. But Nick was hot in a wild, untamed, *rugged* kind of way. He looked like the kind of guy who'd totally blow your back out and you'd thank him for it the next day. Grace was a lucky woman.

Nick stalked up to his wife like a wolf sighting down prey and planted a long, drawn-out kiss on her that gave Delilah enough of a romantic contact high that her knees wobbled. When he pulled back, he grinned down at Grace and said, "I'm shocked you're still standing, angel. How many drinks have you had?"

"Enough to enthusiastically consent to *anything* you want to do to me tonight, but not so much that I'll puke on you," she said, only slurring her words a little.

"The perfect balance," he murmured, then kissed her again.

When the kiss went *well* beyond what was considered fit for polite company, Delilah averted her eyes, feeling like a second-rate, bit player in someone else's love story. She glanced up at

Michael and grinned when she found him frowning at his sister and Nick like he was thoroughly grossed out.

She nudged him with her elbow and whispered, "Nothing like awkward silence between a couple of friends while those around them make out, huh?"

His disgusted frown slipped into a half smile. "Well, if it makes you more comfortable…"

And with that, he gave her an exaggerated duck face and wiggled his eyebrows comically.

The laugh that burst out of her was so wild, so out of control, that she not only sprayed his face with her spit, but snorted when she tried to rein it in.

Awesome.

But Michael didn't seem to care. He simply wiped his face off with his sleeve, his smile growing and his eyes warming the longer he looked down at her.

And the longer he looked down at her like that, the warmer *she* got.

She was *not* going to make it through this event without jumping him. That was just a simple statement of fact.

Next to them, Grace cleared her throat and swung an arm toward her husband, smacking him in the stomach hard enough to make him flinch. "Nick, this is Delilah. Delilah, this is my stupid-hot husband."

Nick held out a hand to her. "Nice to meet you, Delilah."

Delilah managed to not make a fool out of herself as she shook his hand. But that ended when she blurted, "You look like Wolverine's hotter younger brother. Hugh Jackman, Wolverine, that is. Not the comic version, because he was short and hairy and not at all hot. And you're, well, *you*."

D'oh!

Days since last epic embarrassment: zero.

She *really* should have called bumfuzzle on that one.

Nick's eyebrows crept up into his hairline before he glanced back down at his wife. "Did you tell her to say all that to me? Because before you, no one ever compared me to Wolverine."

Grace shrugged. "Delilah's smart. She came to the right conclusion all on her own. I didn't have to say a word."

"Sorry," Delilah said, pinching the bridge of her nose. "The filter between my mouth and brain shuts down when I'm nervous, and family events make me nervous."

Nick grinned the kind of evil, sexy grin Delilah had only seen Captain Hook on *Once Upon a Time* pull off up until that point and said, "Oh, in that case, I think you're going to fit into this family *just* fine."

Everyone got a good laugh out of that. Except for Michael, Delilah noticed. He was looking down at her with an intense expression that made her heart skip a beat or two.

"That's exactly what I was thinking," he murmured.

Gulp.

~

Poor Delilah.

She really does get nervous at family events, Michael thought. He'd assumed she was exaggerating because she was so damned charming when they were alone. But get her in front of strangers and she was a nervous wreck.

Not that it wasn't adorable. But then again, Michael was pretty sure she could belch the alphabet at the dinner table, and he'd still think she was too cute (and sexy and hilarious and awesome) for words.

Michael pulled Delilah aside when Nick and Grace went in

search of appetizers to help soak up some of the alcohol in Grace's system.

"You know there's really nothing to be nervous about, right?" he asked her. "Everyone's going to love you. I can promise you that."

His family was weird and dysfunctional and usually caused a scene when out in public together, but they took well to strangers who were brought into the group by one of their own. Plus, there was Delilah's adorableness to consider. Who the hell could *not* love Delilah?

Other than the tragically nutless, witless, and thoughtless Steve, of course. Stupid fucker.

"Logically, I know there's nothing to be nervous about," she said, biting on her thumbnail. "But I can't help it! Any time I meet a family, I feel like they're judging me. My friends' families all think I'm a weirdo, so do my sister's in-laws. And Steve's family was always judging me—my job, my clothes, my hair, my weight...all of it."

And they always found her lacking, Michael realized.

Steve, wherever you are, you're so lucky I didn't kick your ass in that produce aisle.

He gently grabbed her hand so that she couldn't bite her thumbnail anymore (seriously, the thing looked like it'd been attacked by a pissed off badger) and bent his knees a little so that they were at eye level with each other.

"Delilah, I'm going to be brutally honest with you," he said.

She grimaced. "Ugh. Are you sure you have to? That sounds awful."

See? Adorable. "Yes. I have to. The truth is, you *are* weird. You have a unique point of view about everything, I can never tell what's going to come out of your mouth next, and you're not like anyone I've ever met in my life. I can see why some people would be uncomfortable around you."

She frowned, looking miserable. "Yeah, I know. I'm—"

"I'm not done," he interrupted. "Those people who are uncomfortable around you? They're idiots with a serious lack of imagination and intelligence. Because from where I'm standing? Weird has never looked so good."

Her frown stayed in place while she processed all that, but after a moment, the clouds cleared from her eyes, and she gave him a smile that damn near stopped his heart. "You mean that, don't you?" she asked, her voice husky and full of wonder. "You don't care at all that I'm weird, do you?"

"I do care. I like it. I prefer your *weird* to everyone else's *normal*. Normal is boring."

She shocked the ever-loving hell out of him by leaning in and smiling up at him before whispering, "If this is all part of your plan to separate me from my panties tonight…well, it just might work."

His tongue stuck to the roof of his mouth at that point, so replying wasn't going to happen.

Now all he had to do was get through dinner with his family, the woman who left him at the altar, and a woman he wanted more than his next breath (who was now *clearly* considering moving him out of the friendzone, because she was *flirting* with him)…all with a hard on.

Yep. Seemed about how his luck was running lately.

CHAPTER 12

*A*fter what Michael had said to her, Delilah felt *awesome* about herself.

Until she saw his ex, that is.

She leaned over in her chair and grabbed Michael's arm. "*That's* Sadie? *That's* your ex?" she whisper-hissed.

Michael followed her gaze to the disgustingly stunning brunette on the arm of a tall, muscle-y guy. Delilah couldn't see the guy's face, but she had a *really* good view of Sadie's profile as she chatted with her fiancé in the lobby just outside the dining room. And this woman was *not* what Delilah had been expecting to see.

Or *hoping* to see, she supposed, might be more accurate.

"Yes," Michael confirmed, much to Delilah's disappointment. "That's Sadie. Why?"

Delilah sputtered for a moment. Why? *Why???* "Because she looks like a freaking Disney princess! Like…little cartoon birds pick out her clothes for her every morning."

Then Sadie turned and Delilah got her first full-frontal view of Michael's ex.

"But not old-timey Snow White," she corrected. "Like a sexy, porn-y version of Snow White."

Michael choked on the sip of water he'd just taken. When he stopped coughing, he rasped, "*Porn-y* Snow White? Did you really just say that?"

Delilah frowned at him. He was laughing at her in his head. She could see it in his eyes. He was too polite to laugh out loud, but it was all there in his eyes. "Why didn't you tell me she looked like *that?*"

He raised that smart ass brow of his at her. "Should I be offended you assumed my ex-fiancée would be unattractive?"

"I mean, *of course* I didn't think your ex would be some kind of bridge troll," she admitted. She'd kind of *hoped* she would be, just for the sake of her own self-esteem (which had taken one hell of a beating lately), but she hadn't really *expected* it. "I never thought she'd be a freakin' super model, though."

She was, too. Sadie was probably five inches taller and twenty pounds lighter than Delilah. While Delilah's hair was a crazy rat's nest of auburn curls, Sadie's fell in sleek, shiny, dark waves down to the middle of her back.

And supermodels would be *lucky* to have a face like Sadie's. Knife-edged cheekbones, big, Navy-blue doe eyes, and a pouty, red, Angelina Jolie mouth…Sadie's face reminded Delilah of the really expensive porcelain doll her mother gave her when she was eight.

It'd been the kind of doll that was too pretty and delicate to play with, so it had lived on a shelf in her bedroom, lording its beauty over all the poor, ugly Barbies that Delilah had given haircuts to over the years.

And in this scenario, *Delilah* was the old, abused Barbie with the choppy pixie cut.

It wasn't a good feeling.

Michael had been in love with *this* woman. Had proposed to her. Would've married her if she hadn't left him at the altar. Probably wouldn't have even *met* Delilah, because he would've been at home, *schtupping* his hot wife instead of buying depression supplies at the IGA.

So, Delilah supposed she owed this woman a big thank you...but that would be pretty hard to say while she sat here, feeling about as inferior as she'd ever felt in her life.

"Hey."

Michael cupped her jaw in his big hand and gently tipped her head his way. She swallowed hard when he stroked his thumb over her cheek and grinned down at her. "You're absolutely *gorgeous* when you're jealous."

Well...OK. That helped. Reminded her that *she* wasn't a bridge troll, either, and that gorgeous women weren't competition. She needed that feminist slap in the face, she supposed. But still...

"You could've warned a girl," she grumbled. "I mean, you've seen my ex. You know you're seven *bazillion* times hotter than he is. I could've used a heads-up about your ex, the fantasy porn Snow White."

He gave her a pointed look. "Only *seven* bazillion?"

"Maybe eight," she conceded.

"Michael."

Delilah turned to see that while they'd been talking, Sadie and her fiancé had managed to come up right behind them without her or Michael even noticing. So, not only was she smoking hot, but Sadie was also stealthy like a ninja.

Michael stood up and gave Sadie a hug. "It's great to see you, Sadie."

Sadie pulled back and poked him in the chest with her index finger. "You would've seen me sooner if you'd shown up for the rehearsal."

Michael shoved a hand through his hair and sighed. "I know, I know. I'm sorry. I'm here now, though. Does that count for anything?"

She gave him a wide grin that showed off her toothpaste-commercial white teeth. "It counts for *something*."

Michael offered Delilah a hand and helped her to her feet. "Sadie, I'd like you to meet Delilah Morgenstern. Delilah, this is Sadie O'Connor, soon to be Sadie Montgomery."

Delilah held out her hand, then had to stifle a squeal of surprise when Sadie grabbed it and tugged her into a bone-crunching hug. Who knew that porn-y Snow White was so *strong*?

"I'm *so* glad you're here," Sadie said after she'd released Delilah from her Kung-Fu grip. "After we texted back and forth last week, I just *had* to meet you."

Delilah tried to hide a pained groan, but she wasn't entirely sure she succeeded. "You should know that my grammar is usually better than that. I'd, uh, had a few drinks."

Michael dropped his arm around her shoulders. "*We* had more than a *few* drinks."

Sadie's nose crinkled up as she frowned at him. "And I'll bet she was hungover the next morning and you weren't, right? That's terribly unfair. You need to tell people that before you drink with them. No one should suffer a hangover alone."

"Right?" Delilah said. "So rude."

"Well, if anyone wants to drink tonight, I think it's a safe bet that Grace will be suffering with them tomorrow," a new voice interjected.

That's when Delilah turned and got her first good, long look at Sadie's fiancé, Michael's cousin, the infamous Gage.

"Holy fucking Moses," Delilah blurted. "You're the most beautiful man I've ever seen in real life."

A bubbly laugh burst out of Sadie, and next to her, Michael just sighed and said, "You know I'm standing right here, don't you?"

Meanwhile, Gage just studied her, nearly expressionless, doing little more than a slow blink every now and then.

Delilah slow blinked back at Gage, caught in the tractor beam of his pale, blue-green eyes, but said to Michael, "I mean, you know you're stupid hot. I shouldn't have to tell you that. You've got kind of a Jensen Ackles thing going on. But this..." She paused, shaking her head. "This is a whole other level of beauty. I feel like I'm at the wax museum, looking at some statue that will always look better than the real person because no one in real life is *that* perfect, you know? I mean, seriously, are there any *ugly* people in this family? This is getting weird. And I *really* wish someone would interrupt me. For the love of Betty White, Michael, bumfuzzle! Why don't you ever stop me *before* I hit the bumfuzzle threshold?"

"Because it's entertaining as fuck," Michael said in a well-duh tone that made her want to smack him.

Sadie seemed to take pity on her as Delilah closed her eyes and gave her head a hard shake, trying to overcome the gravitational pull of Gage's damn-near supernatural prettiness.

"It's totally OK," Sadie said. "You're not the first to react like that. For a while, I thought we were going to have to get a restraining order against our neighbor, who insists that Gage looks like the Destiel love child. She draws pictures of him with black angel wings and posts them on her Instagram account. But she quit peeking in our windows, so Gage decided to hold off on legal action. Her art's really good, though. Totally captures the grumpy, broody thing he's got going on."

"Oh my God," Delilah said. "She's right! He *does* look like the Destiel love child!"

Michael snorted. "He probably has no clue what you're talking about."

Gage frowned at him. "I do, too. Sadie made me watch about a million seasons of that show to prove it. But I still don't see it."

He even had Dean Winchester's grumbly, low-pitched voice, Delilah thought. And with his chiseled features and dark good looks, Gage could *totally* pass as the love child of Dean Winchester and fallen angel Castiel.

Frankly, Delilah was still kind of mad at *Supernatural* for not making Destiel happen. And for killing off Bobby Singer. And Charlie Bradbury. And for the entirety of season seven. And the shitshow of a series finale.

But that *so* wasn't the point right now.

She held her hand out to Gage. "I'm really sorry I word vomited all over you. It's nice to meet you, Gage."

He shook her hand and gave her a lopsided smirk that must run in the family, because Delilah had seen the same smirk on both Grace and Michael's faces. "You, too, Delilah."

Then Gage turned to Michael and gave him the standard chin lift that guys did to acknowledge the presence of someone they knew. "Princess," he said.

"Asshole," Michael answered without even a hint of heat.

A dude hug with much back slapping ensued. And seeing the two of them so close to each was both heart-warming (because, *aw*, isn't it sweet that these two guys obviously love each other so much?) and panty-melting (because holy crap, these guys are stunning) at the same time.

"I was serious, though," Delilah said. "Are there any ugly people in your family?"

Gage pulled back and raised a brow at Michael. "You haven't introduced her to Ruthie yet?"

"Who is Ruthie?"

Everyone exchanged a look Delilah couldn't interpret and it made her nervous. *Really* nervous.

So far, she'd embarrassed herself in front of Michael's sister, his cousin, and his ex-fiancée. What was she going to do when she met this Ruthie person and Michael's parents?

Huge gulp.

CHAPTER 13

Once the entire family arrived for dinner, everything went surprisingly smooth.

Well, smooth for Michael's family. For a normal family, it probably would've been deemed a tragic dumpster fire of an event. But for his family, it was like...Tuesday.

As it turned out, the distant family hadn't made it out before the weather hit. That was a blessing. Because while his *immediate* family was dysfunctional, quirky, and not *too* offensive, Michael's distant relatives were, well, kind of scary. They ranged from run-of-the-mill weird to downright sinister, with very little in between.

Michael had been able to talk Sadie out of inviting extended family to *their* wedding, but Gage had apparently let her invite everyone.

Their extended family included third cousins who'd gotten married and hauled their inbred kids around in a minivan with a Confederate flag in the back window above a gun rack, for God's sake. Not *everyone* should get a family wedding invite.

Some of them should remain in the darkest shadows of the family tree *forever*.

So, Gage was either the luckiest bastard on the planet, or he'd sacrificed virgins and goats to whatever gods might've been listening to provide this weather as a gatekeeper to his wedding.

With the scary family snowed in at home, all that remained here tonight was Michael and Grace's parents, Sarah and David, their grandmother Ruthie, and Ruthie's date for the weekend, some gnarled old geezer named Freddie who looked like he was two hundred years old and had a cough that sounded like active tuberculosis.

Sarah was on her best behavior. She'd pestered Grace about when she was going to have another baby, and strongly hinted that Sadie should consider getting pregnant soon. But she'd mercifully stifled any talk of grandkids with Michael.

That was truly the best case scenario with his mom.

He wasn't sure Delilah could've held up under that kind of pressure. Not with her propensity for blurting out whatever she was thinking when she was nervous.

David had barely said anything all night. He probably thought no one knew he had his Kindle in his lap, but everyone did. They all just *pretended* they didn't know he was reading the latest Black Dagger Brotherhood novel under the table. It was easier that way.

Ruthie was, well, Ruthie.

Judging on looks alone, most people would assume that Ruthie was over a hundred years old. She was a living, breathing advertisement for why sunscreen and clean living was important. Years of hard tanning and smoking had left her skin looking like a petrified raisin.

Michael was pretty sure she was shrinking, too. At one time, she'd been five-foot-three. It was hard to tell now because she mostly stayed in her wheelchair (all the better to run over unsuspecting toes with), but if he had to guess, he'd say she was down to five-two.

The blueish beehive hairdo she'd been sporting since 1969 might've given her a few extra inches, though.

But what she lacked in height, she more than made up for in audacity and sheer volume.

For as long as Michael could remember, Ruthie was the loudest, boldest, *rudest* woman in any room. She had absolutely zero concern for anyone's feelings, always said whatever was on her mind, and took shit from no one.

Tonight was no different.

They were on their third waitress of the evening because Ruthie had made the other two cry. Gage had been slipping their current waitress cash any time Ruthie said or did something rude just to keep her on the job. By Michael's count, he'd given the poor kid two hundred bucks so far.

Meanwhile, Ruthie's date was fairly quiet...except for when he'd blurt out loud, random tidbits that had nothing to do with what anyone at the table was talking about. Ruthie said he was deaf as a doornail and too stubborn to wear his hearing aids.

Michael figured that not wearing the hearing aids was a genius move on the old man's part. At least he wouldn't have to listen to Ruthie's story about the torrid affair she'd once had with Abe Vigoda.

Michael shuddered at the mental picture *that* story had put in his head.

And through it all, Delilah sat at his side, seemingly having a great time. It was baffling, frankly. He'd turned to her a few times during dinner to apologize for something Ruthie had said, but every time he did, she had a huge smile on her face and didn't look the least bit offended.

If his family wasn't a turnoff for her, nothing would be.

She was a keeper.

Now he just had to convince her to stick around when all of this was over. Screw the We're Just Friends Accords! It was time to strike a new deal.

"So, Delilah," Sarah said, "How long have you and Michael been dating?"

Delilah glanced over at him and gave him a wicked little smirk before answering, "Sometimes it feels like we only met just days ago. And other times, it feels like we've known each other forever."

Smartass. "We just started dating, mom," he said. "But you know that already. What do you *really* want to know?"

Nick snorted. "Haven't you been paying attention? She wants to know when you're going to start giving her grandkids."

Sarah sniffed delicately as she buttered a roll. "There's nothing wrong with a couple having an honest discussion early on in their relationship to make sure their goals align. I mean, Michael, you want children someday, right?"

"Don't answer. It's a trap," Gage said behind a cough, then blinked innocently at Sarah when she turned a glare on him.

Michael didn't need Gage to tell him his mother's line of questioning was a trap. He'd had this conversation with her many, many times before, and he'd seen Sarah hammer Grace with similar questions for years before she got married and had Ellis. "We're not discussing babies, mom."

"What, is my kid not enough for you?" Grace slurred drunkenly as Nick surreptitiously slid another glass of water her way.

Sarah frowned at her. "Maybe eat something else, dear. I think you've had enough wine."

"Oh, she stopped drinking wine two hours ago," Nick muttered. "She's been doing tequila shots."

"You weren't complaining when I was doing body shots off *you*." She wiggled her eyebrows. Nick shook his head and frowned at her, but his eyes were smiling.

But his sister and brother-in-law doing body shots off each other was *not* something Michael needed to visualize, so he shut that train of thought down with a quickness.

Ruthie tsked. "I told you the Irishman would be a bad influence on her and none of you listened to me."

Nick smiled at her blandly and scratched between his eyes with his middle finger.

"Says the woman who once detailed her sexual fantasies about William Shatner to the entire family at Easter dinner," Gage said, reaching for his own glass of wine and taking a hearty swig.

"And taped footage of her colonoscopy over my wedding video," Sarah grumbled.

"That colonoscopy was more interesting than anything on the entire CBS network that whole year, and now we can watch it again whenever we want," Ruthie said, raising her glass in Sarah's direction. "You're welcome."

Sarah shot her a frown so severe it looked like she might be doing the mental math on where to hide the body and if anyone would alibi her. And Michael had a pretty good suspicion that many, *many* people would be willing to alibi Sarah if Ruthie were to come to an unfortunate end.

Ruthie waved a hand dismissively. "Besides," she began, "you're all missing the point. You're thinking ahead *way* too far into the future, because Michael is nowhere near ready to have babies."

"Thank you," Michael said on a gusty sigh. Then, it occurred to him that Ruthie never helped anyone out of uncomfortable conversations, and he got nervous. "Wait…why would you say that?"

"Because it's clear that you're not even having sex with Dinah over here."

"Delilah," Michael corrected.

"Whatever," Ruthie said with an eye roll. "You're obviously not having sex with her or anyone else."

Delilah leaned forward and rested her chin on her palm, her full attention focused on Ruthie like she was about to impart the secrets of the universe. "How do you know that?"

"The glow." Ruthie swirled a finger around in Delilah's face. "You have no glow. Neither does Michael." She pointed at Grace. "See the glow that one has? The Irishman might not have any scruples, but he has plenty of sperm, and he's giving it to her every night."

"Sometimes multiple times a night," Nick said, completely unconcerned that he'd just been called unscrupulous.

"Amen to that," Grace said, making a grab for Nick's wine, then pouting when he pushed it out of her reach.

"Ugh," Michael muttered. "Chalk that up to stuff I didn't want to ever hear."

Ruthie turned her attention to Sadie. "That one's got the glow, too. See it? Lots of sex."

Sadie blushed to the roots of her hair, but Gage merely smirked, not bothering to confirm or deny Ruthie's claim.

"And you," Ruthie said, pointing to Sarah. Her nose crinkled up as she eyed her daughter-in-law with disgust. "*Tons* of glow. Gross."

Sarah glanced over at David who looked up from his Kindle long enough to wink at her and make her blush as much as Sadie was.

"But *you*," she went on, pointing at Delilah. "No glow. If I had to guess, you haven't had sex in, what, a year?"

"That is *so* not any of your business, Grandma," Michael said at the exact same time Delilah said, "Oh, my God, yes! How did you know that?"

Ruthie shook her head. "You have the same look I had before I met old Fritz over here."

"Freddie," Sarah corrected.

"Whatever," Ruthie said dismissively. "The point is, sometimes a woman just needs to be bent over and banged liked a screen door in a hurricane, and he's the only man in the entire retirement village with a working Johnson. So, I jumped on that right away." Then she cackled at her own joke. "Get it? I jumped on."

"Sweet Christ, there's *yet another* visual I didn't need," Gage muttered, downing the rest of his wine in one gulp.

Same, Michael thought. But he was too hung up on the fact that Delilah hadn't had sex in over a year to voice his disgust.

What the hell was wrong with Steve? It was one thing to break her heart, but to be in a relationship with her and *not* touch her all the damn time? The guy either had superhuman self-control or was the dumbest motherfucker on the planet.

Based on what he already knew about Steve, Michael assumed it was the latter.

"The truth of the matter is," Ruthie went on, "women weren't meant to go for long without orgasms."

Out of nowhere, Freddie blurted, "Not many people know that a male pig can orgasm for thirty minutes. And then..."

He trailed off, then slumped over in his chair.

Sadie leaned forward in her seat and laid a hand on Gage's shoulder. "Is he having a stroke or something? Oh, my God, is he *dead*?"

"Poor bastard has narcolepsy," Ruthie said with a dismissive wave. "He'll be fine."

Gage leaned over and laid two fingers against Freddie's jugular. "Pulse is strong," he confirmed, then went back to his dinner without a care in the world.

Great bedside manner his cousin had, Michael thought. Such a charmer.

As if to underscore Gage's medical opinion, Freddie chose that moment to let out a snore loud enough to wake the dead.

"Aw, that's too bad," Delilah said, slumping in her seat. "I wanted to know what else he was going to say about pig orgasms."

Everyone went quiet for a second or two. Delilah looked around and seemed surprised to find all eyes on her. "What? You can't tell me I'm the only one who was thinking that."

Grace was the first to burst out laughing. Nick followed. After that, the rest fell like dominoes. Even Ruthie chuckled. Michael's cheeks hurt from smiling. He couldn't even remember the last time he'd felt this happy, this hopeful, about anything.

It was official. The We're Just Friends Accords was dead and buried. He would do *whatever* it took to convince Delilah to un-friendzone him, because the alternative was just unthinkable.

If she wanted him even *half* as much as he wanted her, he could work with that.

And if he had his way, if he was the luckiest bastard on earth, her year-long dry spell was going to end *tonight*.

CHAPTER 14

*D*elilah was officially jealous as fuck.

Michael's family was *so* much more fun than her own. Sure, she had that weird second cousin who'd blown his thumb off with illegal fireworks last 4th of July, but other than that, her family was so *boring*. They were all so middle-class, white bread, *average* that she'd always seemed batshit crazy by comparison.

Meanwhile, she fit in *perfectly* with Michael's family.

She'd had a great conversation with David about The Black Dagger Brotherhood and the last Kate Daniels installment. He'd even recommended a few new series that she'd never heard of, making her wish she'd brought her Kindle to dinner, too.

Sarah had promised to teach her how to mend the scarf her grandmother had knitted for her when she was ten. They already had plans for a Zoom meeting/knitting tutorial the following week.

She'd made Grace laugh so hard she almost fell out of her

chair with the story of her drunken penis measuring escapades. Even Nick and Gage had cracked smiles at that one.

Freddie was awesome (when he was awake) and he'd taught her more than she ever thought she'd know about creative embalming techniques (don't ask).

And Grandma Ruthie...oh, Ruthie. She was *exactly* the kind of zero-fucks-given, kickass old lady Delilah wanted to be when she grew up.

Delilah had yet to really bond with Sadie over anything, but that was OK. She'd at least stopped being envious of her perfection. Sadie was the kind of sweet, genuinely good person that usually made Delilah nervous, but she had a welcoming way about her that put people at ease. She could totally see why both Michael and Gage had fallen for her.

And now, with a belly full of the best chicken marsala she'd ever eaten, two glasses of really expensive wine, and a piece of cheesecake so decadent it should be illegal, Delilah was surprised to realize she couldn't even remember the last time she'd had this much fun.

And she owed it all to the man sitting next to her.

She leaned over and whispered, "Thank you so much for bringing me here."

He smiled, leaning in to match her posture. "There's no one else I'd rather be here—or anywhere else—with."

Her gaze dropped to his perfect, pillow-y lips and stuck there. She was an idiot for thinking she could be nothing more than platonic friends with this man. He was sweet, hot, considerate, sexy, nerdy...and he was attracted to *her*.

He was her blueprint for the ideal man, and the only thing keeping her from being with him for real was, well, her. Now she was wondering...what if they started off slow? Maybe a friends-with-benefits scenario?

And after that, what if they did end up being a rebound? Would it be so wrong to rebound with such a great guy? Who said rebounds couldn't last? Couldn't they just keep rebounding for, say, forever?

It could happen, right?

What would Ruthie do? she asked herself.

Ruthie would let the ridiculously hot guy blow the cobwebs out of her vagina. *That's* what Ruthie would do. *Ruthie* wouldn't dither over the decision like a Victorian spinster. She'd grab what she wanted with both hands and never let go.

And it'd definitely take both hands, because ten inches was a lot to handle. Literally. Ahem.

"I agree with you," she blurted, pulling her gaze away from his lips to look him in the eye. "I think we should abolish the We're Just Friends Accords, too."

He looked adorably stunned for a second.

But *only* for a second.

Because right there at the dinner table, surrounded by family, Michael cupped the back of her neck with his big hand, yanked her closer, and growled against her lips, "About damn time."

Then he kissed the ever-loving crap out of her.

Michael's lips were every bit as soft as Delilah thought they'd be—and she'd thought about them *a lot* lately.

He tasted like wine and sin and everything that'd been missing from her life for so long. Someone moaned. It might've been her.

But it didn't matter, because for the first time in *forever*, Delilah felt like she *belonged* somewhere. This place, this family, this man, this kiss—it all felt *right*.

Somewhere in the back of her mind—somewhere far, *far*

away—she knew there was a reason why kissing him *here* and not, say, in their *room*, might be a mistake.

It didn't become super clear, though, until the slow clapping started.

When Michael pulled back and rested his forehead against hers, Delilah was gasping for breath and could barely hear anything over the pounding of her pulse.

But even in her flushed, discombobulated, holy-crap-that-was-the-best-kiss-of-my-life-now-what state, she *did* know it was Grace who had started the clapping that had now made its way around the room. Even Freddie woke up long enough to join in.

Great. She could actually *feel* the blush traveling the length of her body. Her face probably matched her dress perfectly. Not her best look, to be sure.

"I'd say I'm sorry for doing that in front of everyone," Michael whispered, "but I'm not."

She chuckled. "At least you're honest. And a good kisser. That kind of makes the embarrassment worth it."

"Kind of? I'll do better next time."

The way he said *next time* was like a jolt of electricity that shot straight from his mouth into her panties. She'd had vibrators that weren't as effective at hitting her hot spots.

Honestly, if his next kiss was better than his first, she wasn't sure she could survive it.

"That's right, honey," Ruthie said, still clapping. "You get you some Vitamin D. That'll fix you right up."

"Vitamin D?" Sarah asked, sounding confused. "You mean like milk?"

"Oh, fuck," Gage muttered. "Please don't explain it…"

Ruthie cackled. "Vitamin D is what all the kids are calling

dick these days. I'm saying that a good dicking will get the girl back on track and give her a nice, healthy glow."

Gage face palmed and let out an exasperated sigh. "She explained it."

Sarah frowned. "I know I said I wanted grandkids, but I don't really like to think about the specifics of my son *dicking* anyone."

"Well, son of a bitch," David grumbled. "I'm out of charge." He set his Kindle down on the table with a *thunk*. "What the hell are you people talking about now?"

"Don't ask," Sadie and Gage said in stereo.

"Sweet Christ," Nick muttered, reaching for the wine. "I think it's time for me to get drunk, too."

"About damn time!" Grace said. "I was starting to think I'd *never* get you tipsy enough to try on that Wolverine costume I brought."

"Did you know that wolverines are polygamous?" Freddie asked no one in particular. "And in some parts of the world, they're referred to as skunk bears."

That led everyone to a few seconds of quiet reflection before Gage turned to Sadie and said, "And *this* is why I suggested eloping to Vegas."

Sadie bit down on her lower lip and whispered back, "I maybe should've listened."

Meanwhile, Michael's shoulders shook with silent laughter, and Delilah about hurt herself trying to contain her own giggles.

"Still glad you came with me?" he asked.

"Honestly? I can't think of anywhere I'd rather be."

His eyes darkened with what could only be described as raw, primal lust, and Delilah crossed her legs in response. Hard.

"Oh, I can think of *plenty* of other places I'd like to be with you right now," he murmured in a voice that sounded like he'd been gargling broken glass.

Delilah audibly gulped. Yep. There was no way she was going to survive a rebound with this man.

But still...she couldn't think of a better way to go...

CHAPTER 15

*I*t took roughly 700 years for everyone to finish dessert and meander to their rooms for the night. And Michael felt every second of it.

Every. Single. Second.

Because all he wanted was to finally—*finally*—be alone with Delilah.

Everyone loved her, of course. Grace, Sadie, Nick and his mom, had all pulled him aside separately and told him Delilah was a keeper. Ruthie, of course, told him she was far too good for him. Freddie told him something he'd probably never be able to forget about swan mating habits. He shuddered.

And through it all, there was Delilah, charming as fuck, looking like every fantasy he'd ever had come to life.

I think we should abolish the We're Just Friends Accords.

Those words had been running through his mind since they fell from her beautiful, lush lips.

And, seriously, had her lips always been so kissable?

He wanted nothing more than to abolish those damn accords. Obliterate them. Nuke them from orbit.

But he also didn't want to push her.

Well, he *did*. But he *wouldn't*.

He was willing to take it as slow or as fast (*please, oh please, let her want to move fast*) as she wanted. Something told him after everything that'd happened with that fucker Steve, she needed to be in control.

So, he didn't shove her up against the wall and kiss the hell out of her when they stepped into the elevator. And he didn't toss her over his shoulder and throw her down on the bed when they got to their room.

Their room. With its *one* bed.

Michael sighed. If she wanted to take things slow, he'd do it. She was 100% worth the wait...but it'd be painful. Blue balls were no joke, and he'd had them since about two minutes after meeting Delilah.

So, because it would be painful, he sat down on the loveseat in their room, *not* on the bed. He patted the seat beside him. "This seems like as good a place as any to renegotiate the accords."

A nervous giggle burst from her lips as she sat down next to him and smoothed nonexistent wrinkles from her skirt. "I mean, it's not the conference room at Avengers headquarters where the Sokovia Accords were presented, but I guess it'll do."

"We can't all be genius, playboy, billionaire, philanthropists," he said dryly, knowing she'd immediately understand the Tony Stark reference.

She laughed, a little less nervously this time, and settled back in her seat. "Which is too bad, because you'd look *so* hot with Thor hair and a Tony Stark beard."

He thought about telling her she'd look *so* hot in a Black

Widow costume, but thought better of it. Too sexual harass-ment-y for this early in the new accords. That didn't stop his mind from going there, though.

And in his mind, she did look *amazing* in that costume.

So. Very. Hot.

He shifted uncomfortably in his seat and cleared his throat. "Do you want to go first?"

A frown line creased her smooth brow. "I guess I will. But I hope you'll stop me if I start babbling and make things awkward. Or if I embarrass myself. Again."

"Agreed."

"OK." She took a deep breath. "Well, I suppose we should start with how deep we want this not-just-friends-anymore pool to get. Are we talking about casual dating, serious dating, or friends-with-benefits?"

"Yes," he answered immediately. When her eyes widened in surprise, he added, "I want to be with you, Delilah. Casual, seri-ous, or however you'll have me. And, yes, I'm sexually attracted to you." *Understatement of the freaking year.* "So, we'll take things however far you want to go. You're the boss."

Her cheeks flushed as soon as he said *however far you want to go*, which gave him a *big* flash of hope. She was obviously thinking about sex.

He could work with that.

She swallowed hard. "Are you *sure* that what you're feeling isn't…I don't know…heightened because we're here at your ex's wedding?"

"Are you asking if I'm latching onto you because I'm still messed up about losing Sadie?"

She nodded. "I would understand if you are. I mean, she was a big part of your life."

Michael shoved a hand through his hair. "She was. But that

was a long time ago. I don't have any unresolved feelings for Sadie."

Her eyes narrowed like she didn't quite believe him, which made him add, "I'm not saying we don't have any unresolved *issues*. I've been putting off a conversation I need to have with her, which is why I skipped the rehearsal. But that doesn't mean I still *want* her. Trust me, she's where she belongs, and I'm where *I* belong."

Her eyes shifted down to her hands, which she had twisted together in her lap. "See, here's the thing. I like you, Michael. Probably more than I should, considering how little time we've known each other. But I'm fresh out of a long-term relationship, a bad one, and I'm not really sure I'm in a new, *serious* relationship-y place right now. Anything more than casual might be more than I can handle."

If this were a rom com staring Kate Hudson or some shit, she'd tell him she wanted to be with him as much as he wanted to be with her, and then fall into his arms. All the conflicts between them would magically fall away at the 90-minute mark.

But this wasn't a rom com. Michael hadn't really expected her to fall into his arms tonight.

Hoped? Sure. But never *expected*.

He laid a hand over hers and waited until she raised her eyes to his before saying, "I get it. The timing is bad. I can wait. If casual dating is all you're up for, I can live with that."

For now. Not that he wouldn't do *whatever* he could to change her mind.

She shook her head, looking confused. "Why? I don't get it. You can have any woman you want. Why *me*?"

OK, *that* pissed him off a little. He tightened his grip on her clasped hands. "Look, I know that Steve did a number on you and made you feel like you weren't...enough for him. But he was wrong on every possible level, Delilah. You're smart and funny and so damn gorgeous I can't seem to stop looking at you. So, don't *ever* let anyone make you feel like you're not enough *ever* again. Because you're *everything*."

"Wow," she said on a breathy whisper. "That was maybe the best thing anyone has ever said to me."

Steve, you fucking idiot.

He reached out and tucked a loose curl behind her ear. "Stick with me and you'll hear that and more every day."

Michael had meant for the comment to sound lighthearted. But the rusty, rumbly way it came out destroyed any hope of that.

Her pupils dilated as she let her gaze dip to his mouth for a second. "I don't usually have sex with men I'm only dating casually. And I've *never* had a friend with benefits."

And yet she was looking at him like he was a tasty, plated dessert. "Like I said, you're the boss."

Her little pink tongue peeked out as she licked her bottom lip. He had to bite back a groan. She was *killing* him.

"We should probably take it slow," she whispered.

He wasn't sure why they were whispering, but he went with it and whispered back, "I can do slow."

"I meant after tonight," she said. "We should take things slow after tonight. Tonight, I'm pretty sure I need a friend with benefits. Lots and *lots* of benefits."

Then she lunged for him.

CHAPTER 16

*M*ichael was stunned for about two seconds, then rallied and took complete control, fisting his strong hands in her hair, angling her head to deepen the kiss, and stroking her tongue with his.

He tasted so sweet. A little like the wine they'd had with dinner, a little like the cheesecake they'd had right after, and a *lot* like pent up lust and frustration. Not to mention the promise of sin, heat, and multiple screaming orgasms.

It was a giddy combination that made Delilah's head spin, heart pound, and body ache—literally *ache*—for his touch.

Was it possible to *die* from being too turned on? Delilah was starting to wonder.

He pulled back, his breathing ragged, and rested his forehead against hers. He looked like a battle was being waged in his head, and self-control was losing. Badly.

"Are you sure?" he asked tightly.

"So, so sure," she blurted. "You have *no* idea how sure I am."

"Then if you ever want to wear that dress again, you're

going to need to take it off, because I'll shred it if I try," he admitted hoarsely.

She was almost tempted to let him tear it off her. How fucking *hot* would that be?

But this *had* been an expensive dress, so her frugal nature momentarily won out over her lust. Only for a super-short, barely there moment, though, because it only took her half a heartbeat to stand up, yank her dress over her head, and kick off her shoes, so that she was standing in front of him wearing nothing but her black lace bra and matching panties.

Her thighs trembled as he slid his big, warm hands over them. When he grabbed her hips and lifted his eyes to hers, the raw, primal need she saw there gave her pause. It'd been a long time since she'd had sex. What if it wasn't good for him?

She wasn't really concerned that it wouldn't be good for her. It was a safe assumption it would be *amazing*. She was so turned on right now that he could probably sneeze on her and make her come.

"You're so damned beautiful."

His voice was so awed, so full of wonder, that it brought tears to her eyes. She was sure that no one had ever wanted her as much as Michael wanted her in this moment, and every last insecurity she had vanished.

They were going to be *so* good together. And when this was all over, they'd probably both be ruined for anyone else. And at the moment, she couldn't even contemplate why that might be a bad thing.

That knowledge gave her the confidence to sassily ask, "Well, are you going to stare at me all night, or are you going to get naked?"

~

If he lasted three seconds when he got inside her, it'd be a miracle.

He'd known that the minute she took her dress off and he got his first look at her flawless, lace-wrapped curves and smooth skin. Then she'd mouthed off snarkily and *that* turned on him even *more*. If that was possible. He was fairly sure he could've pounded nails with his hard-on *before* he saw her half naked. Now…someone could get hurt if he wasn't careful.

"Oh, I will," he told her, tightening his hold on her hips and dropping to his knees in front of her. "But this isn't about me."

She bit her lower lip as his breath fanned across her bare stomach. "It's not?"

"Nope."

He slid one hand up her back and gripped the delicate edge of her panties in the other—and in a slick move he'd probably never be able to replicate, he unhooked her bra with his index finger and ripped her panties off with his other hand in stereo.

She gasped and looked down as her torn panties hit the floor and her bra slid off her shoulders to join them. "Holy shit," she said, her voice trembling.

"Sorry," he murmured. "I'll replace those."

"Not necessary," she said.

At least that's what he *thought* she said. It was kind of hard to tell over the ringing in his ears, which he assumed was caused by all the blood in his body rushing south of his belt.

Sweet Christ, her breasts were perfect—round and full, and just the right size to fill his hands. Every inch of her was nothing short of spectacular.

He was going to have to paint her at some point. Not that he could do her justice…but he had to try. She was living, breathing art, and it would be criminal to *not* try and capture her beauty on canvas.

Hell, if he could write poetry or songs or limericks...*anything*...in honor of her body, he would.

But that was something to think about later.

Much, much later.

His brain locked up for a second. There was *so* much territory he wanted to cover here. He wanted to map out her entire body with his hands and tongue, learn what it took to make her gasp and moan and come and beg for mercy.

But where to start?

That's when she rubbed her thighs together, squeezing them tight, and suddenly he knew *exactly* where to start.

She whimpered at the first brush of his thumb over her clit. Gasped when his tongue followed the same path. Trembled when he slid first one, then two fingers inside her, stroking her g-spot while his tongue flicked against clit over and over again.

Delilah hooked one leg over his shoulder, digging her heel into his back, and he manfully held in a whimper of his own. He really had *no* idea how much longer he was going to be able to last without being inside her.

Not much, was his guess.

But he refused—*refused*, damn it!—to go *anywhere* until she came, so he grabbed her ass with his free hand to hold her steady while he got to work.

Her entire body started shaking as he worked her over with his fingers and tongue, and her hands alternated between combing through his hair and tugging on it helplessly as she got closer and closer to her inevitable climax.

The sounds that started falling from her perfect lips were guttural, animalistic, and loud enough to do *amazing* things for his ego. And she'd called out his name enough that by now, everyone on their floor probably knew it.

She was so, *so* close. He could feel it in the tightening of her muscles and hear it in her raw voice.

"Yes," he murmured. "Let go. Come for me, sweetheart. Now."

And much to his immense pleasure, she did.

Her every shudder, every inner contraction and convulsion, was a gift—a gift he intended to draw out of her time and time again before this night was over.

He let out his own grumbly, growl of satisfaction that meshed perfectly with her broken cries and moans, and nothing had *ever* sounded better.

When the last of her shudders subsided, she dropped her leg from his shoulders and threatened to slide bonelessly to the floor.

Nope. Not gonna happen.

Michael stood up, neatly upending her over his shoulder along the way, and walked her over to the bed. She giggled when he dumped her in the middle unceremoniously.

And he was really glad he hadn't put her down gently, because the way she bounced was *magical*.

In that moment, looking down at Delilah's dreamy, sated smile, Michael knew this was as close as he'd ever get to being a superhero. His superpower was making Delilah Morgenstern come, and that was perfectly fine with him. He'd take Delilah over x-ray vision or flying or teleportation any day of the week and twice on Sundays.

Then she sat up on her knees, scooted to the edge of the bed and reached for him. He immediately got lightheaded and was pretty sure he heard a choir of angels begin singing the *Hallelujah Chorus* when she deftly undid his pants and dragged them down to his knees, along with his boxer briefs.

He kicked his way free of the pants and briefs and tore his

way out of his shirt. Buttons pinged all over the room. He couldn't care any less. All that mattered right now was Delilah.

And right *now*, Delilah was looking at his hard-on like it was a juicy steak and she hadn't eaten in months.

Again, talk about doing *amazing* things for his ego. He was pretty sure the awe on her face alone made his cock grow two extra inches.

Michael stroked a hand over said cock, then shook his head as he started moving toward her. "Delilah," he managed on a ragged exhale.

Her eyelids fluttered at the sound of her name on his lips, and she backed away slowly, dragging herself up to the head of the bed. She leaned over and grabbed a condom from her purse on the nightstand.

But she didn't hand him the condom like he expected. No, that just wasn't how Delilah's brain worked. Instead, she laid it on the bed and shoved on his shoulders until he flopped onto his back.

The grin she shot at him when she slid down his body was pure sin. "My turn," she all but purred.

He let out a needy sound that was nowhere *near* cool.

He'd always known that one night with Delilah would ruin him for other women. But he hadn't considered the possibility that he might not survive it. That intense pleasure might be the death of him.

But he was sure as *hell* considering it now.

CHAPTER 17

*M*ichael's eyes were a little glazed over, his lips parted in surprise, as she took his rock-hard cock in her mouth and tipped her eyes up to his.

He choked out a harsh breath and watched her cheeks hollow out as she sucked him harder. His hand slid into her hair and tightened reflexively. He was *barely* hanging on to control. She could feel it in his thigh muscles, which trembled as she worked the length of him with her mouth and hands.

"Fucking hell, Delilah," he muttered through clenched teeth. "You're killing me."

She'd never swallowed before. She wondered idly if he'd give her a heads-up (literally) before he came. Or if he'd just...

That's when he pulled back, giving her hair a gentle tug to get her to let go. "Did I do something wrong?" she asked.

"Fuck, no. I just can't take much more of that. I'm about to lose control."

She bit down on her lower lip. "What if I want you to lose control?"

She gasped when he flipped her over onto her back like she was weightless and deftly rolled the condom on.

"Ladies first," he said with an evil grin.

Her heart pounded a staccato tattoo on her ribcage and her brain was a cluttered, jumbled mess of thoughts that amounted to little more than *YippeeYippeeYippee*.

Michael crawled up her body slowly, stopping only briefly to give her breasts the attention they were practically begging for.

All the while he held his weight off her in that way that men did when they were afraid of crushing a woman. And his gaze was so open and so full of emotion it made her feel *needed* in a way she'd never felt before.

She felt tears pricking at her eyelids at the intensity of it all, but then he smiled down at her—a smile so full of sex and sin and sensual promise that her mind blanked.

All she could do now was feel…and she felt *glorious*. Desired. Powerful. So, so powerful.

He nuzzled her nose with his as he settled himself between her legs. "You're sure?"

She nodded, shifting her hips restlessly. "I might die if we don't. I've never wanted *anyone* like I want you right now. Please, Michael. I need you."

A tremor ran through him at her words. Then he took pity on her and finally—finally!—started sliding into her, inch by glorious inch.

And she was now 100% sure that her drunken measurements had been right, because there were *a lot* of hot, hard, throbbing inches sliding into her right now. If he hadn't already made her come once so hard she felt a little dehydrated, she might not have been able to accommodate his size at all. Not easily, at least.

After all, she hadn't had sex in so long that her hymen had probably miraculously healed itself—like an earring hole closing up after months of not wearing earrings.

She let out a guttural moan when he filled her completely. "Oh, God, you feel *so* good."

His neck muscles flexed as he took a deep breath. He was holding back, she realized. Probably trying to make it last.

Well, fuck that. She didn't want his restraint. She wanted wild, unbridled, swing-from-the-chandelier passion. She wanted to drive him crazy, to make him completely lose it and fuck her like a rutting beast. *That's* what she wanted. That's what she *deserved*.

Delilah grabbed his face between her hands and made sure she had his full attention before saying, "Stop holding back. You need to fuck me *now*. Hard. If I can walk straight tomorrow and sit down comfortably, you haven't done your fucking job. Do you understand me?"

The throaty sound that escaped him at her words made her shiver. "Fuck, yes."

Then he grabbed her leg, hooked it over his hip, and *really* started to move.

Delilah clawed at his shoulders and arched her back. "Yes," she hissed. "God, yes."

He gave her exactly what she'd begged him for. In and out, slowly at first, then harder and faster. In and out, in and out, until he pushed her knees up and angled even deeper.

"Michael…" she moaned.

He slid an arm under her hips and lifted her, so that the base of his cock hit her clit with every thrust.

Her moans hit such a fevered pitch that people two counties over could probably hear her. She reached up behind her and gripped the headboard, holding on for dear life.

"Oh, please, don't stop. Don't stop!" she chanted.

"Christ, Delilah," he said, sounding like his jaw was clenched so tight it might crack. "You need to come. Now."

He was on the edge, she realized, but God bless him, he didn't stop or slow down. He just went harder and faster, giving her everything she needed.

Then he slid his hand down her chest, over her stomach, down, down, down, until his thumb unerringly found her clit. That was all it took. She broke with a scream that was louder than a gunshot in the otherwise quiet room.

Every muscle in her body tensed, her toes curled, and her vision went blurry. *That's* how hard she came.

And he still didn't stop.

He did, however, pull out long enough to deftly flip her onto her hands and knees before slamming into her again. His hands shifted up to her breasts, pinching her nipples. Hard.

She was so surprised, so turned on, that another orgasm hit her out of the blue. And *that* was all it took to push *him* over the edge.

Michael buried his head in her hair and came with a possessive growl that was so sexy it would've made her come again if she wasn't already completely, utterly, wonderfully, sated.

And dehydrated, most likely.

Delilah collapsed onto the mattress as Michael rolled off her and disposed of the condom. She wondered how he'd even found the strength to do *that* much. The effort he'd just expended to make sure she came three times (to his once) was nothing short of miraculous.

She shoved a hank of sweaty hair out of her eyes as Michael flopped down next to her and trailed his fingertips up and down her back. "Holy crap," she whispered. "That was *amazing*. Like, I'm pretty sure we could go pro."

Michael pushed up on his elbow, then leaned over and kissed her forehead so gently she wanted to cry. "Nah, I'm good with maintaining our amateur status. You know, just in case fucking ever becomes an Olympic sport. That way we still have the option of going for gold."

She snorted. "Well, you'd win for sure. That was definitely a gold medal-worthy performance."

"That was all you, sweetheart."

She shook her head. "No way. I've had sex before. That was some next-level orgasming."

His eyes darkened and he smiled an evil smile that promised all manner of dirty things before he grabbed her and lifted her so she straddled him. "It might've been a fluke," he said. "We'll only know for sure if we're able to repeat it."

She sputtered, ready to protest that she couldn't possibly go again, but when he lifted his hips and she felt him getting hard again—already!—she changed her mind.

Best. Friends. With. Benefits. Rebound. Ever.

CHAPTER 18

The next morning, Delilah felt like she was seeing the world with new eyes. Everything looked brighter, smelled better, and seemed more hopeful.

Grandma Ruthie had been right. It was *amazing* what Vitamin D could do for a girl's outlook on life.

She was contemplating the breakfast buffet, trying to decide between a doughnut and a croissant, when Grace sidled up next to her and mumbled something that vaguely sounded like, "Morning."

Delilah grinned at Grace's dark glasses, disheveled hair, and the visible whisker burn on her throat. "Well, good morning, sunshine."

Grace groaned. "Not so loud!"

She winced in sympathy. "Hung over, huh?"

"No," Grace said in a voice just barely pitched higher than a whisper. "I've been hung over before, and this is something way, *way* worse."

Delilah nodded. Been there, done that. "Regrets?"

To her surprise, Grace cracked a smile. "Not a single one."

Vitamin D, Delilah thought. *When you're right, you're right, Ruthie.* "Maybe you should try and eat something," she suggested.

She'd gone to McDonald's after her last (and final, by God) hangover and ordered the greasiest breakfast known to man. It'd fixed her right up.

Grace looked at the buffet over the tops of her glasses and gagged a little. "There's no way. But I didn't come over here for the food. Sadie needs help."

"Oh, OK. What's wrong?"

Grace sighed. "It'd be easier to tell you what's *not* wrong. But, long-story-short, the roads are being taken care of now that the snow stopped, but the wedding planner can't get here in time for the ceremony...and neither can the stylist, make-up artist, photographer, minister, and a huge majority of the guests."

Yikes. Delilah had worked with more brides than she could count, and most of them were already stressed to the point that one minor thing going wrong could send them over the edge. She'd never seen a situation where *everything* went wrong before. Sadie must be a nervous wreck. "How is Sadie?"

"That's the weird part," Grace said. "She's...calm. Like weirdly, eerily calm. Mom's with her now and we're trying to get everything figured out so that we don't have to reschedule, but we could use your help."

Delilah grabbed the doughnut *and* the croissant as she followed Grace to Sadie's room. Something told her she was going to need the extra sustenance to get through *this* day.

~

After last night, Michael had been fairly sure there was nothing sexier in the world than Delilah, naked and under him, moaning while she came. While he used his superpower and *made* her come.

He was wrong.

As it turned out, watching Delilah take charge of an insane, all-out clusterfuck and wrangle it into submission was by *far* the sexiest thing he'd ever seen in his life.

"Are you *sure* you don't want to reschedule?" she asked Sadie and Gage. "If your wedding planner is any good at all, she'll be able to reschedule everything with no problem."

Sadie bit her lip and looked up at Gage.

Gage slid his hand under Sadie's hair to cup the back of her neck, then leaned down so that they were eye-to-eye. "I would've gone through the drive through at the Elvis chapel in Vegas if that's what you wanted," he said. "I'll marry you anywhere, anytime, with everyone watching, or with no one watching. Whatever *you* want to do is fine with me. I'm the luckiest bastard in the world to be marrying you, so I'm not about to complain about one ceremony. I care about the *marriage*, being the best husband I can be, not the wedding."

Sarah honked into her handkerchief. "Oh, Gage, that was lovely."

"Oh, quit your blubbering," Ruthie grumbled. But even her eyes looked suspiciously moist as Sadie smiled up at Gage.

"I'm marrying you *today*," Sadie whispered. "I don't want to go through another *minute* not being your wife."

Michael was pretty sure he'd never seen his cousin smile like he was now. He'd been so mad at Gage for so long because he'd managed to win Sadie's heart, but seeing them together, this happy, made Michael's feelings seem completely trivial.

He'd never really had *that* with Sadie. She'd never looked at him like she was looking at Gage—and vice versa, if he was being totally honest with himself. They'd been dumb kids *playing* at being in love. What Gage and Sadie had—*that* was the real thing.

Sadie deserved to be truly, deeply, madly loved, and Michael knew beyond a shadow of a doubt that Gage was the right man for the job.

In this case, the better man had clearly won.

It kind of made him feel like a dumbass for ever thinking Sadie was his one and only shot at happily ever after.

His gaze immediately went to Delilah, who was smiling at the happy couple, her eyes soft and dreamy.

And that's when it hit him. Shit, if they were in a cartoon, this was the point where a giant lightbulb would start flashing above his head.

Even though everything between them was tentative and new, his heart knew what his head had been too stubborn to admit up until this point.

Delilah was more than just a keeper. She was The One.

She was everything he'd ever wanted, everything he'd been *sure* he'd never find. And after last night, she'd officially ruined him for all other women, because even though she'd been insistent on only having a friends-with-benefits relationship in the short term, he was abso-fuckin'-lutely sure he'd never experienced better *benefits* in his life. And never would again.

Now all he had to do was make *her* see that.

Easy, right?

With his luck?

Not fucking likely.

CHAPTER 19

*O*nce Gage and Sadie made it clear they were going through with the wedding come hell or high water (which really might happen, given everything else that had gone wrong so far), Delilah *really* went to work.

First, she helped David get ordained online so that he could perform the ceremony. The whole process was beyond simple and took all of fifteen minutes to complete.

The hardest part had been convincing Ruthie that Freddie wasn't up to the task of performing a wedding ceremony. But when Delilah reminded her that David had the deeper, more church-y voice, she reluctantly backed down.

Delilah wasn't about to let Freddie officiate and run the risk of him passing out before he could get to the vows. Or of incorporating animal husbandry facts into the ceremony.

Then, she let the kitchen staff know they could go ahead and prepare all the food as planned (it'd just go bad, otherwise), but that the entire resort staff was invited to the reception so they could minimize the waste. But even so, there would still be too much food, so Delilah made arrangements with the local soup kitchen to pick up all the leftovers.

The concierge called in his sister, a hair stylist and make-up artist, who lived close by and drove a four-wheel- drive truck, so getting through the snow wouldn't be a problem for her.

Although, once Delilah showed the woman a picture of Sadie, she didn't think the entire National Guard would keep her from getting her hands into that gorgeous, thick mass of dark waves. Sadie was a hair stylist's wet dream. Delilah was their nightmare.

But that was another story entirely.

One of the housekeepers on staff was an amateur filmmaker and had agreed to act as videographer. Delilah watched a documentary the woman shot about the day in the life of a hotel mattress, and once she got past the horrifying content, she could admit the film was beautifully shot.

(She'd probably never be able to sleep on another hotel mattress, though. Yikes.)

Delilah would take the photos, of course, which was really the only thing Sadie seemed to care about. She'd even insisted on paying her for her time, which Delilah ignored. She was here, she was happy to help, and she would *not* be taking this happy couple's money.

She wouldn't tell them how lucky they were that their original photographer couldn't make it, though. The woman Sadie had hired was charming and a born salesperson, but her work wasn't anywhere near as good as Delilah's, if she did say so herself.

The floral arrangements had been delivered the afternoon before, but no one made it in to place them today, so Sarah was busy handling that. Delilah had no doubt she'd do a great job after David showed her a photo of the greenhouse he'd built for

Sarah the previous year. To say Michael's mother had a way with flowers was like saying the ocean was a tad wet.

So, two hours after she was brought in, everything was blessedly in order.

Bad weather: 0. Delilah Morgenstern: 1.

Now, there was only one thing left to do. Unfortunately, that one thing was a task she'd been putting off all day.

But there was no avoiding it now.

Delilah took a deep, fortifying breath and knocked on the door to the groom's ready room. Nick opened the door, looking all kinds of amazing in his tux. He smiled at her before saying, "Hey, Gage, your hero is here."

She laughed. "Shh, I'm just a mild-mannered wedding photographer by day. Can't let you expose my secret superhero identity."

He stood back and ushered her in with a deep bow. "Your secret is safe with me, milady."

Gage stood in front of the mirror, futzing with his tie. He was muttering under his breath like Yosemite Sam, too. Lots of grooms did that. In Delilah's opinion, there should be classes for grooms. Tying the Damn Tie 101 would be required.

She stepped in front of the mirror and brushed his hands out of the way. "Let me."

"Thanks," he mumbled.

"You're welcome. I have to talk to you about something."

"Whatever Sadie wants is fine with me," he said on autopilot.

She chuckled. "Oh, you're going to be a great husband. That's 100% the right answer."

"I can confirm," Nick said from his position leaning against the doorframe.

"But this is *for* Sadie," she said as she wrestled his tie into submission. "See, your dad was going to give her away. But now, he's officiating."

Gage shoved a hand through his hair. "Fuck."

Delilah nodded. "Yeah. I mean, it's not like she *needs* anyone to give her away. But, after talking with her earlier, I get the idea that she was kind of excited to have someone walk her down the aisle, you know?"

He nodded thoughtfully. "She was. Her dad was…not a good guy."

Nick snorted. "Understatement of the fucking year."

"So, I'm afraid that having her walk down the aisle alone might be a sad reminder of how…" Delilah trailed off, searching for the right words.

"Unbelievably shitty her childhood was?" Gage supplied helpfully. Bluntly…but helpfully.

"Yeah, that. My thought was that Nick should walk her down the aisle."

Nick straightened up and grinned. "Fuck yeah, I will."

She grinned back as she finished with Gage's tie. "I thought you'd say that. But you already have a job at the ceremony."

"Best man," Gage murmured. "I think I see where you're going with this. You think I should ask Michael to be best man."

She nodded. "What do you think?"

Nick winced. "That's kind of an awkward ask, isn't it?"

"Yes," she agreed. "But a necessary one if you want to have a best man. And for the pictures, trust me, you want a best man, especially since Grace is maid of honor. Without a best man, the photos won't be as balanced." As Gage's frown deepened, she hastened to add, "But if you're really against it, I can make the pictures work. I just thought—"

"No," Gage interrupted. "You're right. If the bride was

anyone else, he would've been my first choice for best man, anyway."

"Thanks, man," Nick said dryly. "That's heartwarming."

"Oh, fuck off," Gage snapped. Then his expression softened as he turned back to Delilah. "I'll ask him. Thank you. For everything."

She patted his now perfect tie. "Don't thank me until you ask him. It might turn out to be the worst idea I've ever had."

She could only hope Michael wouldn't hold it against her when Gage asked him to be his best man. When he married Michael's ex-fiancée.

But if he was as over Sadie as he claimed to be, he'd probably be fine with the whole thing...right?

"Hey, princess."

"Asshole," Michael answered on autopilot.

Gage had been calling him princess since he was just a kid. It used to annoy him. He always assumed that's why Gage did it. But now that he pretty much expected it and Gage *still* did it, he figured the nickname was going to stick for all eternity.

Michael had a quick mental image of himself at ninety years old, sitting in a nursing home next to a similarly ancient Gage as they yelled insults at each other at top volume because both of them were as deaf as Freddie.

Michael sneezed as he placed a gigantic vase full of...some kind of flowers in the corner of the chapel, per his mom's orders. "I guess Mom forgot that I'm allergic to this shit when she asked me to help her."

"She gets the two of us confused sometimes. She thinks I'm allergic to flowers and that you hate cauliflower," Gage said.

"I love cauliflower."

"And I think it's the work of the devil."

Michael shook his head. "When she was really mad at me when I was a kid, sometimes she'd yell at me and accidentally call me Gage."

Gage half-smiled. "That's because I was always the one in trouble. It was an easy mistake to make."

"Yeah, I can see that." He flicked his gaze over Gage in his tux. "You clean up OK."

Gage gave him a similar once over. "And you don't look completely ridiculous dressed up, either."

"Aw, stop it. You'll make me blush."

Gage rolled his eyes. "I need a favor."

Huh. Gage hadn't asked Michael for a favor since he was fifteen and needed an alibi for when he skipped school and went to Atlantic City with a college girl who called herself Cinnamon. But something told him this wasn't going to be *that* kind of favor. "Shoot."

"So, Nick *was* best man, but now that your dad is officiating and won't be able to walk Sadie down the aisle, Nick's going to do that, which means…"

Gage trailed off, rubbing the back of his neck. Michael could make it easy on him and let him off the hook.

But, nah. That wasn't their style.

Michael blinked at him innocently. "So, you've finally come to the realization that *I'm* the best man? About fucking time, man."

Gage punched him in the arm, but only put about twenty percent of his strength behind it. Michael knew it was only about twenty percent because he'd definitely taken Gage's best punch a time or two in the past, and this one *wasn't* it.

"Will you be the fucking best man or not?" Gage grumbled.

Five years ago? He would've said no way. Hell, two years ago, he would've said no way. But today? "Yeah, man, of course I'll do it," he said quietly.

Gage almost smiled. You could tell by the slight twinkle in his bluish green eyes. An almost smile from Gage was like a standing ovation from anyone else. "I would've asked you first, you know. I wasn't sure how you'd feel about it," Gage admitted. "I didn't want it to be weird for you."

Michael shrugged. "I mean, yeah, it's weird. But we're a weird family, so I say we roll with it."

"We *are* weird. That's for fucking sure. It's amazing *anyone* wants to marry into this family."

Michael winced. "I probably should have picked a more entry level dating event for Delilah rather than tossing her into the center of the three-ring circus."

Gage chuckled. "You did kind of flash her all the crazy at once. But I think she can take it. She's weird, too. In a good way. You better lock that down."

Oh, he intended to. No matter what. Because not locking it down, letting Delilah walk away, taking all her beautiful weirdness with her, was unthinkable.

CHAPTER 20

$\mathcal{D}$elilah didn't get a chance to talk to Michael before the ceremony, which bugged the crap out of her. She would've loved to make sure he was OK with being best man *before* having to see him standing up there.

Gage had said they were "cool", but in this case, "cool" could've meant anything from everything is actually fine and had been worked out in a grown-up manner, to "a fist fight *probably* won't break out on the way to the alter," to a million things in between.

Gage wasn't what anyone would call an overly communicative sort.

But she didn't have time to think about that for long, because the ceremony started right on time.

Delilah didn't know what Michael was feeling, but through her camera lens, standing at Gage's side, he certainly looked the part of a dutiful best man who wasn't going to object at any point during the ceremony.

And he looked *fuck* hot in the tux she'd literally stolen off of

Nick's body for him.

But that was beside the point.

In the end, despite all the chaos leading up to the event, the ceremony itself went off without a hitch.

Sadie, of course, was breathtaking in a simple, vintage-looking gown. She'd opted for no veil, and let her hair fall in loose curls down her back.

The concierge's sister had come through in a *big* way on her makeup, too, which was tasteful, understated, and lovely—just like the bride.

Gorgeous, stoic, perfect Gage had teared up when he caught sight of his bride to be, walking toward him on her brother's arm. He'd probably deny it later, so Delilah made sure she captured the whole thing on film.

Nick didn't tear up as he gave away the bride, but he wanted to. Delilah could tell.

Grace, despite what was probably the worst hangover in existence, looked lovely in her tasteful, off-the-shoulder, lavender bridesmaid gown.

David was the *perfect* officiant. His deep, resonant voice carried to the back of the chapel, where Sarah didn't even *pretend* to hold her tears back, Ruthie honked every so often into a handkerchief she'd pulled from her bra, and Freddie snored gently.

Sadie and Gage opted for a traditional ceremony (without the word "obey", of course) and didn't recite custom vows, but they didn't need them. The look of pure, unadulterated adoration and love in their eyes as they spoke the standard vows was more powerful than any other words would've been.

And when David pronounced them husband and wife, the kiss Sadie and Gage shared was hot enough to melt the stained glass in the chapel's windows. Delilah got all *that* on film, too.

More photos followed, which Gage *hated*. Getting him to smile was a Herculean task—but Delilah was more than up to the challenge. He wasn't the first camera-shy groom she'd photographed. She quickly learned that all she had to do to get a natural smile out of him was to have him look at Sadie before she took the photo.

It also didn't hurt that he was *stupidly* photogenic. His bone structure was truly a gift from the gods.

But now that she had a gazillion perfect photos of Sadie and Gage, Nick and Grace, and the entire family together (plus all the individual shots), she wanted a few of just the guys—a generational shot. So, she carefully placed David, Nick, Gage, and Michael together in front of the gorgeous stone hearth in the resort's lobby.

"Alright, guys, last couple of shots," she told them, framing the shot. "You're hanging in there like champs. OK, I'm ready, so look at me and think about what an awesome photographer I am, and how thrilled Sadie is going to be with these shots." They chuckled, and she added, "Or, you know, you could think of how happy this occasion is. Whatever works for you."

The next ten shots were so perfect she didn't even bother to take more. She dismissed everyone. Gage practically left a smoking trail in his wake like the Road Runner in the old Bugs Bunny cartoons.

Michael put his hand on her back as she scrolled through the shots. "You've got to be exhausted," he said. "You worked your ass off today." Then he leaned down and whispered in her ear, "And you didn't get much sleep last night."

Having his warm breath skate across the shell of her ear did *naughty* things to her libido. It also stirred all kinds of dirty, *dirty* memories of all the other places on her body his breath had touched the night before. She shivered. "And whose fault is *that?*"

"Mine," he answered, not a trace of apology in his tone. "And you better get in there and get something to eat. You'll need your strength, because I have *no* intention of letting you sleep tonight, either."

And with that, he swaggered off as if he hadn't just set her panties on fire.

Now, how the hell was she supposed to go in there, take reception photos, and pretend she wasn't completely distracted?

The man was diabolical.

And you're falling for him.

Trouble was, after all the fuss she'd made about not wanting to rebound, and about how she wasn't ready for a serious relationship and couldn't handle anything beyond a casual, friends-with-benefits scenario at the moment, she had no idea how to tell him how wrong she'd been. And if she *did* somehow work up the courage (or blood alcohol level) to tell him, would he still feel the same?

He'd said he wanted a real relationship with her, but that was before they'd had sex. Maybe he was perfectly happy with just sex now?

Was she just heading for yet another epic rejection?

Delilah resisted the urge to bang her head on the wall.

How the hell did she manage to get herself into these messes?

What she really needed now was a plan. Surely there was a way she could gauge his interest before making a complete fool of herself. Again.

"I guess we'll soon find out," she muttered to herself as she headed into the reception.

CHAPTER 21

*A*s everyone loaded their plates at the buffet and Gage left the table to get Sadie a drink, Michael knew *this* was the moment he'd been waiting for. He'd been procrastinating long enough.

If he wanted a real future with Delilah, he had to settle his past. And to do that, he needed to talk to Sadie.

With the deepest of resigned sighs, he approached her table. She looked up at him and smiled the kind of sunny smile only someone who was truly, deeply, blissfully happy could smile.

She waved him over and gestured to the empty chair Gage had vacated. "Sit down," she said. "Keep me company while my husband tries to avoid talking to anyone at the bar." Then she shook her head and put her hands on her flushed cheeks. "That sounds so weird. My *husband*. I don't know if I'll ever get used to that."

He chuckled. "I mean, I don't know. I think we were all pretty surprised that *anyone* was willing to marry Gage. The grumpy bastard."

Her grin was all kinds of conspiratorial as she said, "He would never let on, but underneath all that gruffness, he's really just a big teddy bear."

Michael loved Gage like a brother, but he was *no* teddy bear. "I'll have to take your word on that one. Sadie, I've wanted to talk to you for a long time."

Her smile slipped and she looked nervous for a second. "Michael, if this is like the last time—"

"Oh, shit, no." He held up his hands in supplication. "I promise. I'm not about to profess my love and try to win you back."

Not again, anyway.

On the night that Grace's daughter, Ellis, was born, Michael had seen Sadie there, holding the newborn, looking all motherly and familiar and like...*home* that he'd lost his mind temporarily. He'd also been fresh off a breakup and not in a very good place emotionally.

But that was a different story.

The point was, he'd been stupid enough to try to kiss her, even while it was clear that she was 100% over him and 1000% in love with Gage. The whole debacle had ended in a fistfight with Gage and a few hours in the drunk tank at a downtown police station for both of them, with Ruthie (of all people) showing up to bail them out.

It had been a humiliating and humbling experience (jail wasn't something he ever wanted to repeat. He didn't even speed anymore, just in case), but also an enlightening one. That was the night he realized that he needed to let go of his anger, move past the hurt feelings, or else he was going to end up bitter and alone.

"I owe you an apology," he said. "I've owed you an apology for a long, long time."

Her brow crinkled up. "Is this about the scar on Gage's

cheek? Because honestly, it's kind of hot. Keeps him from being too pretty."

Michael had gotten in a lucky shot during his fistfight with Gage that resulted in a tiny scar on his cousin's cheekbone. In return, Gage had punched him in the kidney and he'd pissed blood for three days.

Good times.

"No," he said, "I apologized to Gage for the scar. He doesn't seem to mind it, either. I owe you an apology for…shit, this is hard to admit."

Sadie grabbed his hand. "Whatever it is, it's OK. We're good. You don't have to say anything else."

It was just like Sadie to give him an easy out. To let him off the hook. Well, he wasn't going to let her do it. Not this time.

He didn't deserve it.

"I was a shitty boyfriend to you and an even worse fiancé. I was selfish and self-absorbed and you deserved better. I had my head so far up my own ass that I ignored what was wrong between us. I mean, you weren't entirely happy, even before you met Gage, right?"

She opened her mouth, then shut it, obviously searching for the right words. That was Sadie. Always so damn careful to never hurt anyone's feelings.

"It's OK," he told her quietly. "You can say it. I already know."

"Yes," she admitted. "I had been unhappy for a while. I didn't know why, and it didn't have anything to do with you—not really, anyway. I was unhappy with *me*. And I was just so desperate to be part of a family that when you proposed, I pushed all my misgivings to the side and went with it, you know?"

He nodded. He *did* know. That was why he'd proposed when

136 | ISABEL JORDAN

he did. He'd sensed her pulling away and offered her the one thing he knew she'd never turn down: family. He'd used her weakness against her.

Which made him the worst kind of manipulative asshole imaginable.

It was a secret he'd carried all these years. He'd let her and Gage carry the blame because that was easier than admitting he'd manipulated a woman he was supposed to love and care for just to selfishly keep her at his side.

"I knew you'd say yes when I asked you to marry me—not because you were crazy in love with me, but because you wanted a family more than anything. I was so afraid of losing you that I used your need for a family as something to anchor you to me. Like a fucking albatross around your neck. It was selfish, manipulative, and wrong. I'm so, so sorry, Sadie. Can you forgive me?"

She tightened her hold on his hand and leaned in closer so that he was forced to raise his guilty eyes to hers. "Michael, seriously, you have *nothing* to apologize for. You were a dumb kid. We were *both* dumb kids. You're *supposed* to make stupid, selfish mistakes when you're a kid. And in the end, you *did* give me everything I ever wanted. If you hadn't brought me home with you, I wouldn't be where I am today. And I'm so happy, Michael." Her eyes filled with tears. "I can't even tell you how happy I am. On some level, I have *you* to thank for that happiness."

He let out a shaky laugh. "Wow, that's a generous interpretation of events."

She shrugged delicately. "What can I say? I'm in a generous mood." Then her expression grew more serious as she added, "You were my first love. You'll always hold a very special place in my heart. I can forgive all the stupid mistakes you made when you were a kid for that alone—if you can forgive mine, of course."

"I can," he answered without hesitation. "Of course, I can. Thank you so much."

She yanked him in for a hug. "Any time. We're family now, after all."

"We've always been family, Sadie. Always."

CHAPTER 22

*D*elilah sat at a table in the very back of the reception hall and watched Michael and Sadie with unblinking interest—all while trying to pretend to *not* watch them. They were obviously having a moment, and she had nothing to do with it. She had no business watching them.

And yet, here she was, with her eyes glued to everywhere he was touching Sadie (and vice versa) as they hugged.

It shouldn't hurt. She knew that. Sadie was now a happily married woman. Nothing was going to happen between her and Michael ever again.

What she didn't know was whether he'd ever feel for her what he'd once felt for Sadie. Was he even capable of loving her like he'd loved his former fiancée? Would she always be his second choice?

And *that's* what hurt. The not knowing.

She was jerked out of her pathetic musings when a shot of tequila was plunked down in front of her. "Oh, I didn't order this."

Gage sat down next to her with his own tequila. "But you need it. I can tell."

"How can you tell?"

"Because I've been where you are." He gestured with his chin to where Sadie and Michael were still huddled together. "There was a time when I was watching the two of them together, wondering where—or even if—I fit into all...that."

She couldn't help but smile at him. "You seem to have figured it out."

He snorted. "Not on my own. Sadie had to set me straight—while I was in a jail cell after Michael and I were arrested for brawling in a hospital waiting room like a couple of dumbasses."

Now *there* was a story she hadn't heard. She started to ask for more detail, but he held up a hand and said, "But that's not the point."

Good stories didn't always need a point. Freddie had taught her that much. But she didn't really know Gage well enough to argue with him, so she let it go. "What is the point, then?"

He shoved a hand through his hair, looking a little uncomfortable. "Look, I don't get involved in people's personal lives. Romantic...*shit* isn't anything I want to discuss with people. Ever."

Wow, now *that* seemed like an understatement. "I could sense that about you."

His grin was something that could be weaponized against horny women everywhere. It should come with a loud, blaring warning of some kind. Maybe he should wear caution tape around his neck? "You're a smartass," he said. "Perfect for Michael."

She let her gaze drift back to where he was still deep in

conversation with Sadie. "I'm not entirely sure he feels that way," she said quietly.

"That's why I'm here, talking about shit I do *not* have any desire to talk about. See, Michael and Sadie were each other's first loves. What they have...it's something we'll never be able compete with."

Delilah frowned at him. "You weren't kidding. You really *aren't* good at talking about this stuff, are you?"

He rolled his eyes and gave her the finger, which would've made her laugh if she was in a better mood. But she wasn't, so she didn't.

"What I was going to say before I was fucking rudely interrupted," he added dryly, "was that it's *fine* that they have this thing we'll never have with them. Because what *we* have with them is different. First love is rarely ever the permanent kind. Our kind? What I have with Sadie and what you're building with Michael? *That's* the permanent kind. So, the past doesn't matter. Not at all."

She bit her lip. "Well, that's clearly true for you, but Michael and I...we just aren't there yet. Maybe one day..."

He narrowed his blue-green eyes on her. "Yeah, I figured you'd say that. And I figured you'd be a stubborn ass about it, because that's exactly the way I was when I was in your position. It took Sadie spelling it out for me like I was a two-year-old before I finally got it. But I grew up with Michael, and he can be pretty dumb, so I didn't trust *him* to spell it out for you. That's why I'm here."

"Well, OK. Explain it to me like I'm a two-year-old, then."

He looked so smug he reminded her of Michael for a minute. "Oh, I can do better than that. Did you get a picture of Michael's face when Sadie was coming down the aisle?"

It was a little insulting that he had to ask. "I got pictures of *everything*."

"Look at it."

With a sigh and *no* idea where he was going with this, she picked up her camera and found the best picture she'd taken of Michael when Sadie was walking down the aisle toward Gage.

He looked happy. Almost...proud. No jealousy or sadness or misgivings—not even a trace. She sniffed and reluctantly admitted, "OK. Now I see where you're going with this."

"Kid, that isn't even the half of it. Now, pull up the picture of him with me and Nick and David. The one where you told him to look at you."

She did as she was told and pulled up the best of the shots she'd taken of all the Montgomery men together—and what she saw made her gasp out loud.

Gage laid a hand on her shoulder as he stood up to go back to his bride. "I'm betting if you look at pictures of my face when Sadie was walking down the aisle and Nick's face when he saw Grace, the look on *Michael's* face when he's looking at you is pretty similar."

Holy crap, he was right! The look Michael was giving her was a completely different look than the one he was giving Sadie, and it didn't have anything to do with the dirty, hot sex they'd had all night long. Well, not *everything* to do with it, at least.

There was a softness in his eyes, almost like wonder. Awe that she was there and that she was his—even if it was only in some tiny way. Even after she'd insisted that they stay a casual thing and take things slow.

Casual. She was *really* starting to hate that word.

"He's crazy about you," Gage went on. "So, why don't you cut him slack and tell him you're crazy about him, too, huh?"

Her answering snort of laughter was a little watery. His grip tightened on her shoulder for a split second before he added, "Now, let's forget this ever happened, huh? Because I *really* don't want to be the one you come to in the future for advice when Michael acts like an asshat."

"Nope," she said, not willing to miss the opportunity to rib him a little. "I'll *never* forget it. And I'm going to tell everyone how sweet you were to me and what great, *romantic* advice you gave me."

He cringed as he turned to leave. "I'll fucking deny it to my dying breath," he muttered. "And *no one* will believe you."

"Hey, Gage?"

A deep, world-weary sigh. "Yeah?"

"Thank you."

That earned her a tiny, barely there smile. "Welcome to the family, kid."

She was still bathing in the warm knowledge that Michael was as crazy for her as she was for him when another voice hit her like whiff of hot garbage baking in the summer sun.

"Dee? Thank God I found you. It took me *forever* to get here."

No. Fucking. Way.

Slowly, she turned in her seat and looked up into the face of the very *last* person she wanted to see at this event. The last person she wanted to see *anywhere*, actually.

"Steve. What in the cinnamon toast *fuck* are *you* doing here?

CHAPTER 23

*A*fter talking to Sadie, Michael felt like thousand-pound weights had been lifted off his shoulders. He'd had no idea just how much all those years of guilt for being such a lousy boyfriend/fiancé to Sadie had weighed on him. With amends made, it was finally time to move forward. And there was only one person he wanted to move forward with.

Too bad she was nowhere to be found.

Guests who'd managed to brave the weather had started to trickle in after the ceremony, but still, the ballroom wasn't terribly crowded. Finding her shouldn't be this hard. Where the hell was she?

He went over to where Grace and Nick were dancing—well, more like slow swaying, actually, because he imagined Grace's hangover was still wretched—and tapped Grace on the shoulder. "Have you seen Delilah?" he asked over an incredibly nauseating instrumental version of *Lady in Red*.

(Seriously, why did wedding reception music always have to

be so *awful*? This crap was barely a step above elevator and grocery store music.)

"She was over in the corner taking pictures a minute ago," Grace said, frowning at the empty corner where Delilah had apparently once been. "Maybe she went to the restroom?"

"I saw her talking to Gage while you were talking to Sadie," Nick offered.

Grace and Michael both blinked at him. "Like, *Gage* initiated a conversation—or like, she had him cornered and was forcing small talk on him?" Grace asked.

"He approached her," Nick said. "So, I'd say he initiated." When they continued to blink at him, he added, "He's not *feral*, you know. I'm not sure why everyone is so surprised when he opens his mouth."

Well, Michael supposed *feral* probably was an exaggeration. Especially since he met Sadie. *Semi*-feral was closer to the truth.

But still, he couldn't imagine Gage saying anything to her that would upset her or make her leave.

Just then, Ruthie rolled up, dragging Freddie behind her. "She's not in the can. I was just in there and other than a skinny chick with gas bad enough to clear a Taco Bell, it was empty."

"That's...graphic. Thanks, Grandma," Grace said dryly.

Ruthie waved her off. "I saw Darcy leave about five minutes ago with some guy."

"Delilah," Michael corrected with a frown. "What guy?"

She shrugged. "I dunno. Looked like a pencil-dicked turd to me. You should go get her. Check the lobby."

"You're bigger than he was," Freddie added helpfully. "You could definitely take him in a fight."

Michael was going to thank him, but Freddie slumped over where he was standing. Nick caught him and eased him into a folding chair before he could hit the ground.

"Well, damn," Ruthie said, shaking her head at her fallen date. "Looks like I'm not getting laid. He'll probably sleep the rest of the night."

And on that note...

Michael headed toward the lobby, forcing himself to walk, not run. Who the hell would she have left with? He hoped she wasn't in some kind of trouble.

"If you punch the guy out, keep your thumb on the *outside* of your fist this time!" Ruthie shouted after him. "You don't want to break it again!"

"Son of a bitch," he muttered. "That was *one time,* and I was ten."

Didn't anyone in this family ever forget anything?

Delilah hadn't seen Steve look like *this* in years.

He was disheveled—and not in the cool, sexy way that Michael looked when he first got up in the morning. The look Steve had going was more of an I-stayed-up-all-night-mainlining-caffiene-and-candy-to-study-for-the-physics-final-that's-75%-of-my-final-grade thing.

Not that Delilah had ever done that. Ahem.

His hair—which didn't appear to have a drop of gel in it—was standing up everywhere. He had bags under his eyes that were big enough to store his girlfriend's giant plastic boobs in, and his clothes looked like they were last week's wrinkled rejects that'd been plucked off the floor for round two or three wear.

And he'd driven through a snowstorm, to a resort where he knew no one and had no business, to find her. His ex. The woman he'd unceremoniously dumped over a month ago.

What the *hell* was going on? And more importantly…

"How did you even find me?" she asked.

He cleared his throat and shoved a hand through his hair. "Well, remember when you were taking that night cooking class in the sketchy part of town?"

She resisted the urge to roll her eyes. Every part of town that wasn't his was "sketchy" to Steve. "Yeah, why?"

"I put a tracking app on your phone. You know, in case you got into trouble."

No. Fucking. Way.

"You *tracked* me here?" she said on an angry, violent hiss, like a cobra about to strike. "Like I'm a lost *dog* or something?"

Or, more like he was a crazy *stalker* or something.

He held his hands up in supplication. "I know it's a violation of your privacy, and I'm sorry. I was just desperate."

"Why? What on earth do we have to talk about that's *that* important?"

Steve had the nerve to look her in the eye, and say, with unnerving sincerity, "Us. I made a huge mistake, Dee. I love you and I want you back."

Now *there* was a plot twist she hadn't been ready for. "No, seriously," she said dryly. "Why are you here? Did you finally figure out I stole one of all of your brown and black socks from each pair so that you'd never have a match?"

His jaw dropped. "I *knew* someone took those from the laundry! I blamed Mrs. Johnson in 4C." Then he shook his head and said, "That's not important now. I'm being serious, Dee. I love you. I miss you so much."

Probably because he had nothing in common with his little fuck toy, who was much younger than him. Why was it that men were always surprised that younger women didn't *get* them? "That's not my problem, Steve. We broke up. We both moved on. It's over. You need to go. And take the damn tracking app off your phone."

He set his jaw mulishly. "I'm not going anywhere. I *didn't* move on, not really. And neither did you."

Well, she had the sore inner thigh muscles and ripped panties to refute *that* claim, but she didn't see the point in making that argument. "What makes you so sure?"

He had the nerve to laugh. "Oh, come on. We both know this guy is *not* your type."

Her eyes narrowed on him. If he knew what was good for him, he'd run now. But he obviously didn't. He just stood there like a dumbass when she said, "And what makes him *not my type*, Steve? The fact that he's amazing looking, kind, and always puts my needs ahead of his own? Is *that* what makes him *not my type*?"

"It's just...well, a guy like that is never going to be a long-haul guy. Not with a..."

He trailed off, but it was clear where he was going. "Not with a girl like me," she finished for him.

Again, he had the audacity to look relived that she seemed to follow his train of thought. "Right. He's not like us, Dee. He's the high school jock type. The kind of guy who stuffed kids like *us* in our lockers. He'd never understand your *quirks*."

His tone made having quirks sound like a flaming case of genital warts. "Not like *you* do, huh, Steve?"

He nodded, and she wondered idly if he'd file charges if she nut-punched him. Surely once she told this story to a jury, they'd say it was a justifiable assault, right?

But she kept her fists to herself, just in case. No need to tempt fate. This asshole just wasn't worth it. "But you *didn't* tolerate them, did you? Toward the end of the relationship, everything I did, said, or wore seemed to embarrass you. You made me feel...less than. And you know what? Not *once* has Michael *ever* made me feel that way. He looks at me like I'm the most gorgeous, delightful woman in any room. He *celebrates* my weirdness and doesn't *ever* try to change me."

That's when it hit her like a brick between the eyes.

She'd been keeping Michael outside her emotional wall because of how *Steve* had made her feel about herself. He'd pricked little holes in her self-confidence, and she let him do it. And when she had a chance to really move on and make things official with Michael, she'd held back out of fear, thinking—on some level—that she wasn't good enough for him.

Well, *fuck* that.

Steve looked furious, like he was barely holding his temper and jealousy in check, but she couldn't bring herself to care as she poked him in the chest with her index finger. "You know what, Steve? He's *not* too good for me. I'm a *great* catch and you treated me like garbage. So, no, you will *not* be getting another chance with me. You can turn on the little slime trail you made when you crawled in here and follow it back home, because we are *done*."

"A-fucking-men."

Delilah whipped around as Michael approached, giving her a slow clap. "Couldn't have said it better myself," he said, giving Steve a serious stink eye.

She bit her lip. "How much of that did you hear?"

"Enough of it to tell you how right you are."

Steve snorted. "Sure. You're going to try to tell me that your *relationship*—for lack of a better word—is real. That someone like *you* is going to date someone like *her* long term."

Michael only had eyes for Delilah as he said, "I'll be what-ever she needs for as long as she'll let me, and that'll make me the luckiest son of a bitch who ever lived."

Delilah's breath caught in the back of her throat for a second. "I was so afraid of rebounding and getting hurt," she said in a near whisper. "But now, I realize that *this* asshole is nowhere near the guy he was when I started dating him. He's a completely different person. So, if anything, I rebounded with *him* on my way to *you*."

Michael grinned at her. "Well, that's a pretty big stretch, but I'll take it if it means I get you in my arms even a *second* faster."

It did, too. She lunged at him. He caught her easily, swinging her up into his arms. Her legs automatically went around his waist as she kissed the crap out of him.

When she broke the kiss and rested her forehead against his, she took a huge gulp of air before saying, "I don't want to do casual anymore. Casual is *crap*. I want formal. Super formal. Like, date nights and going steady and you meeting my family and us going to bingo night at Ruthie's retirement home and sex all the time."

He kissed the tip of her nose so gently it brought tears to her eyes. "Super formal sounds pretty damn good to me. Except for Ruthie's bingo night. That shit can get dangerous."

She laughed. "But not dating anyone else is good?"

His eyes darkened with lust and passion and longing. "Nothing has ever sounded better. I'll warn you upfront. I've always been a shitty boyfriend. I *will* make mistakes, and there will probably be times that you consider smothering me in my sleep with a pillow. But I swear to you, no one will *ever* try harder to deserve you than I will. And I'll do *whatever* I have to do to make you happy, because I'm falling for you in a *big* way, Delilah Morgenstern."

Oh, shit, he really *was* going to make her cry! "I'm falling for you, too," she said, her voice raspy from all the joy clogging her throat. "And I can *guarantee* you'll want to smother me with a pillow at times, too. Probably after I've used all your razors to shave my legs, and clogged the shower drain with my hair."

"I'll buy more razors. And a drain snake," he promised.

"My hero," she murmured before catching his lush bottom lip between her teeth.

"Ugh," Steve groaned. "This is it, Delilah. I swear, if I leave now, we're done. Do you hear me?"

"Is he still here?" she asked Michael.

"I don't hear anything," he answered, slanting his mouth over hers once again.

And after Steve stormed off and they found the nearest coat closet with a locking door, neither of them heard anything but the combined sounds of their pleasure for a long, long time.

CHAPTER 24

*W*hen they walked back into the reception hall later (slightly sweaty, disheveled, spent, and smiling ear-to-ear), the party was in full swing. The hotel staff was drinking, dancing, and laughing, and so were the guests who'd braved the snow to be there.

Grace and Nick were sitting at one of the tables in the back of the room, making out like a couple of kids at the prom. David and Sarah were on the dance floor, showing the younger couples how it was done. Sadie and Gage were at their table, and she was talking animatedly about something while he listened intently, a small smile curving his lips.

Ruthie and two of the children in attendance seemed to be decorating Freddie with flower garlands, paper chains, and fairy lights while he snoozed in a corner. The kids squealed with delight with every decoration they placed, and Ruthie cackled, looking happier than Michael had ever seen her.

All in all, this day he'd been dreading for months had turned out to be the happiest he'd had in, oh, maybe *ever*.

And he owed it all to the gorgeous, quirky, hilarious, whip-smart woman at his side.

He slid an arm around her shoulders, pulled her in close, and pressed a kiss to the top of her head. "Are you happy, Delilah?"

The smile she beamed up at him was damn near blinding. "I've *never* been happier."

He kissed her, putting every ounce of joy and lust and longing he felt for her into it, and she gave it all back to him with the kind of unbelievable, open generosity that he'd come to realize was just pure Delilah.

She didn't know it yet, and he wasn't about to tell her for fear of scaring her off, but he was going to marry her. One day…he was going to marry her.

Of *that*, he was certain.

Michael was so wrapped up in Delilah and his plans for the future that he barely noticed the commotion going on around them.

Until a bouquet smacked them upside the head.

They broke their kiss to glance down at the bundle of flowers that'd bounced off their heads and landed at their feet.

Well, if *that* wasn't a sign from the wedding gods, he sure as hell didn't know what was.

That's when he noticed all eyes were on them.

Grace had picked up Delilah's camera and was snapping pictures. Sadie—who'd apparently just tossed the bouquet—and Nick were clapping, while his mom was wiping tears of joy from her eyes. Hell, even Gage was giving him a thumbs-up.

He shifted his gaze back down to Delilah and he raised a questioning brow at her.

Her laugh ended in a snort that made him smile even harder. "Don't even think about it," she said.

Too late, beautiful. "Well, when *can* I think about it?"

She pursed her lips like she was deep in thought, then said, "Not for *at least* a year. And all this isn't anywhere *near* my dream wedding, just so you know. My dream wedding might be too weird even for you."

A year. He could work with that.

"I guess we'll find out, Delilah."

Let the countdown begin…

EPILOGUE

EXACTLY ONE YEAR, TO THE DAY, TO THE *MINUTE*, LATER...

*D*elilah was seriously regretting her costume choice.

The Rey costume (*The Last Jedi*-era Rey, of course) had seemed so perfect when she'd picked it out. But now, standing outside the Star Wars convention in the cold, waiting for Michael to show up, where non-nerds were giving her serious side-eye, the whole thing seemed like an epically bad call.

She had no idea why he'd insisted on meeting her here. She could've waited for him to finish up at school and they could've driven here together, she thought grumpily.

If only she'd decided to dress as *The Empire Strikes Back*-era Princess Leia. *She* had a coat.

And why the hell had he wanted her to wait *outside* for him?

She could be inside where it was all nice, cozy, and nerdy, but no. Michael had been *insistent* that she not go in without him.

It's not like he ever asks too much of you, her inner nice girl told her inner grumpy bitch. *He gives you whatever you want. Why not just stand out here and wait without complaining?*

Easy for her inner nice girl to say. *She* wasn't out in the cold in a scavenger costume.

But that didn't make Inner Nice Girl any less right. Michael *was* the perfect boyfriend.

They'd been living together for the past six months and he did the dishes without being asked, never let his dirty socks miss the hamper, and always, always, *always*, made sure their orgasm ratio was at least three-to-one in her favor.

Could a girl really ask for more than that?

And that's when she saw him coming toward her and her heart did a little leap. She might've thought she was having a heart attack if her heart didn't do that *exact* same leap every time she saw him.

She grinned as she noticed his costume. He could've come dressed as Kylo Ren like the thousands of others she'd seen going into the convention, but no. Michael was Ben Solo, complete with the black sweater with the hole in it where Rey had stabbed, then healed him.

And he looked *fuck* hot, as usual.

Then her gaze shifted, and she noticed he wasn't alone.

His entire family was with him...in costume.

Sadie was there in a very elaborate Padme, *Revenge of the Sith*-era costume that just barely concealed her hugely pregnant stomach. Grace was there in a *The Empire Strikes Back*-era Princess Leia costume.

Grace really *was* the smartest.

Nick was there, too, in a Mandalorian costume, holding little Ellis who was, of course, Baby Yoda.

Ruthie rolled up in a Darth Vader costume, followed by Freddie in a truly *great* young Luke Skywalker outfit.

Gage was in…blue hospital scrubs. She wasn't surprised. He was way too cool for cosplay, she imagined.

When Michael stopped in front of her, she shook her head and asked, "What is going on? What are you all doing here?"

He cocked his head to one side and grinned down at her. "Don't you remember telling me about your perfect, weird, wedding day?"

Her heart stuttered and her mouth went dry.

No. Fucking. Way.

She'd laid out her perfect wedding for him about a month after they'd moved in together. *The Star Wars* con, surrounded by friends and family, cosplay, and an ordained Yoda.

She swallowed hard. "Are you saying…"

He grabbed her hand and got down on one knee. "Delilah Morgenstern, you completely ruined me for all other women, and I've been crazy, stupid in love with you for over a year now. I don't want to go another *minute* without being your husband. But I'm afraid that I'm a package deal. All these crazy assholes behind me are part of the deal. So, if you agree to marry us and make me the luckiest bastard who ever lived, my dad's inside, in a Yoda costume, ready to marry us. Your mom and sister are in there, too. If it's too soon and you want to wait, I understand. But if you'll have me…"

Whatever he was going to say next ended in a strangled *oomph* as she tackled him to the ground and kissed the hell out of him.

"Yes," she murmured against his lips in between kisses. "I'm so in love with you, I can't stand it. So, yes, I'll marry you right here, right now, you crazy bastard."

"Thank God," he said, cupping her face between his hands and kissing her back with everything he had.

"Can we go inside now? It's colder than a witch's tit out here," Ruthie grumbled.

And *splat* went the romance.

Michael stood up, pulled her to her feet, then kept her tucked against his side while they got hugs and well-wishes from the family she'd just agreed to marry into. She glanced into the convention center and saw her parents waving wildly and her sister giving her a hearty thumbs-up.

"I adore you," Michael whispered in her ear. "You know that, right?"

She let out a teary chuckle. "Since you're here, at a Star Wars convention, in a Ben Solo costume, getting ready for what's *sure* to be the weirdest, nerdiest wedding ever, I'm going to go with *yes*."

"Well, this isn't really the complicated part," he said. "Wait until we start talking about bringing *kids* into this three-ring circus."

Oh, God, the babies they'd have would be so beautiful his mother would *cry*. But instead of saying *that*, she said, "I'm not even going to *talk* about babies for at least a year."

His eyes lit up in a way that suggested he clearly remembered her saying that exact same thing about when she'd be ready to talk about marriage.

"I can work with that, Delilah. I can work with that."

Keep reading for samples of The Has-Been and the Hot Mess,

a snarky, sassy contemporary romantic comedy, Semi-Charmed (the paranormal romance that started it all), and Caped and Dangerous, the first book in my Grumpy Superheroes series. Happy reading!

ACKNOWLEDGMENTS

Writing is a lonely job. Pouring stories and characters that only exist in your mind onto paper is HARD—and no one can do it for you. But that doesn't mean that anyone can write a whole book and get it published without support. Here's mine:

- My husband and son who never let me down and do whatever they can to help protect my writing time
- My parents who do even MORE to protect my writing time than my husband and son do (sorry, guys, but it's true)
- L.E. Wilson who provides more technical support and emotional support than I can even fathom. Seriously, why do you tolerate me?
- Dar Albert who somehow manages to turn my vague, totally unhelpful direction into book covers
- The ladies in the Bitch, Write Faster fan group for always being SO understanding about the fact that I'm the world's slowest writer.

I couldn't do what I do without all of you, so, from the bottom of my heart, THANK YOU!!

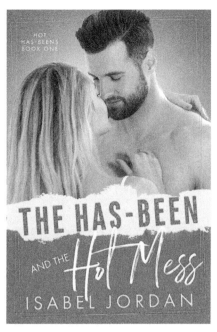

Her job is to resurrect his image. Falling for him is not part of the plan...

CHAPTER 1

Whoever said sleeping with the boss was a bad idea was wrong. It was when you *stopped* sleeping with the boss that the trouble really started.

Kendall Quinn flopped down on the couch next to the battered cardboard box that now represented the remains of her career. Four years as a PR manager with the most prestigious talent representation agency in LA and all she had to show for it was an over-watered Philodendron, a half-eaten container of Tums, and a severance check that wouldn't even cover her half of next month's rent.

She kicked off her heels and tossed her iPhone on the coffee table, not bothering to check for messages. Kyle had almost certainly made sure no one would try to contact her—none of her clients, none of her coworkers. She was well and truly screwed.

Metaphorically, of course. Because to add insult to injury, Kyle had been a lousy lay. Bastard.

It wasn't even like she could turn around and sue him for

wrongful termination. Even though he'd all but *admitted* he'd fired her because it would be uncomfortable for his new girlfriend to have to work with her every day, Kendall had failed to bill the required number of hours for the past two months, which was the official party line for why she'd been terminated.

And as far as party lines went, it was super credible. Especially since she recently lost her biggest client to the hateful little bitch—her protégé, no less—who'd also stolen Kyle from her, making it nearly impossible to bill the required monthly hours.

Getting new clients took time, too. Wining, dining, schmoozing, and convincing Hollywood types to trust her with their precious PR, social media, and crises management wasn't an easy task. It *especially* wasn't easy for someone like Kendall, who had very little control over the filter between her brain and her mouth, which was why she'd lost Lynsay Storm, country music's flavor of the month, as a client in the first place.

But that wasn't worth thinking about right now. It was done and there was no going back. What she needed now was a plan for how to recover from this fiasco.

First and foremost? She needed a new place to live. Kyle had given her a month to vacate the townhouse they shared. The miserable asshole didn't even have the decency to offer her the place as a parting gift, which was just spiteful, seeing as he was staying with his new fuck toy.

She also needed to figure out what she was going to do for work. Because apartments in LA didn't just magically pay for themselves.

She wished she could pull a *Jerry McGuire* and try to convince some of her old co-workers and clients to follow her. But the non-compete she'd signed when she was hired by

Walker and Patrick PR was iron clad. If she tried to steal any of their clients and employees now that she was a free agent— even though that status had been forced on her—she'd pretty much owe a kidney and her firstborn to the firm's lawyers.

Even if she could find a way to weasel out of her non-compete, it wasn't like any of her clients would leave Walker and Patrick for her. Sure, her clients liked her, but Kendall was sure they loved the firm's endless resources and connections even more.

Honestly, until she ran the out the clock on her non-compete (five years, if she remembered correctly), the best she could probably hope for here in LA was occasional consulting work, or finding brand new, awesome, unrepresented talent.

And finding brand new, awesome, unrepresented talent in this place? Her odds of finding a unicorn with the Holy Grail shoved up its ass were better. Practically every waiter and wait-ress with a dream and a modicum of talent had representation here in La La Land.

Sweet crap on a cracker, what had she gotten herself into? Had she really lost her career over a douchenozzle like Kyle Walker?

It didn't escape her attention that nearly every mistake she'd ever made in her twenty-nine years of life could be traced back to a good-looking, smooth-talking, dark-haired, bad-boy asshole.

Losing her virginity at sixteen to a guy who'd told the entire school she'd given him crabs when she broke up with him? Yep. That'd happened. Vance McNeil—quarterback of the football team and hotter than he had any right to be, with hair and eyes the color of melted dark chocolate.

Then there was the bartender with the deep, grumbly bari-tone and midnight eyes she'd dated for two weeks. That relationship had come to a screeching halt when she found out he'd stolen her jewelry and pawned it to pay off his gambling debts.

Kyle was no better. He hadn't stolen from her or told the entire office she was an STD-ridden whore or anything, but he'd done something much worse. He'd actually tricked her into thinking he was a good, decent guy. The kind of guy who, despite his gorgeous face, olive-toned skin, and wavy chestnut hair, would never fuck her protégé on his desk where anyone could walk in and find them only weeks—WEEKS!—after asking her to move in with him.

Gah! Her taste in men was shit. Her next boyfriend would be a blond with absolutely zero alpha tendencies, by God.

Kendall jumped when her phone rang, then she lunged for it. With any luck, Kyle had realized he'd been a short-sighted jackass to fire her and that there was no way he could keep the agency going without her.

She sighed with disappointment when she realized it wasn't Kyle calling. But hey, at least this caller was a blond. Maybe her luck was starting to turn already.

"Hi, Ray," she said, trying not to sound like a defeated, pathetic, desperate loser. "It's not a good time. Can I call you back later?"

After I've eaten the giant bag of cheese puffs I bought on the way home and washed it down with a cheap bottle of wine?

She could practically hear Ray rolling his blue eyes heavenward. "Oh, please, Ken Doll," he said. "I know you're about two seconds away from carb-loading and binge-watching *The Great British Baking Show*. You have nothing better to do than talk to me."

"Rude," she grumbled. True, but rude, nonetheless. "And don't call me Ken Doll. You know I hate that."

"Whatever you say, pumpkin."

Pumpkin was only marginally better, but she'd allow it. "I was fired less than an hour ago, Ray. How do you already know about it?"

"Your ex-protégé," he said. "I called your office because you weren't answering your cell and she spilled the beans. Gleefully, I might add. She has absolutely *zero* discretion."

"Yeah, I kind of figured that out when I caught her banging Kyle on his desk yesterday at lunch," she said dryly.

And she'd only caught them because she'd felt bad when he told her he had to work through lunch, so she'd picked up his favorite sandwich—chicken salad on rye—from Joe's deli where they usually ate lunch together.

But apparently all he'd *really* needed for lunch was Tiffany bent over his mahogany desk with her skirt shoved up to her waist and her thong around her ankles while he fucked her from behind as hard as he could manage with his pencil dick. Asshole.

Ray let out a disgusted sound. "Ugh. I knew I hated that guy as soon as he said *The Rise of Skywalker* was the best *Star Wars* movie ever. There is no one on earth less trustworthy than a straight white guy who loved that movie more than *The Empire Strikes Back* and *The Last Jedi*. Dumb motherfucker."

Kendall knew better than to engage in a *Star Wars* discussion with Ray. It was a never-ending rat hole that often led to him asking if she knew anyone who could get him a meeting with JJ Abrams so that Ray could kick him in the shins.

So instead, she just sighed and said, "I should've known Kyle was too good to be true. Tiffany, too. It was at least partially my fault for trusting the wrong people. Again."

"I knew neither of them would last."

"And now you're psychic? Great," she said, her voice

completely devoid of emotion. She held up her middle finger. "Tell me what I'm thinking right now."

He chuckled. "Oooh, feisty. I like 'em feisty."

"That would be great for my ego if I didn't also know you like 'em male."

This time he let out a sharp laugh that actually made her smile. But only a little. "Baby," he said, "if you were a dude, I would've married you by now."

Now that one hurt a little. The closest thing to a marriage proposal she'd ever had, and it was from her gay best friend. "Good to know that if I only had a penis, I'd be married and employed."

"'If I only had a penis'…the forgotten song lyrics that never made it into the final cut of *The Wizard of Oz*," he quipped.

Kendall shook her head. "Funny. You're a funny guy, Ray."

"Oh, buck up, buttercup. It can't be as bad as all that. Why did the asshole fire you, anyway?"

"The real reason? He thought it would be awkward for his new fuck toy to have to keep reporting to his *old* fuck toy every day. The made-up reason? I lost the Storm account."

"Well," he said, "you *did* call her a brainless twatwffle. On national television."

Kendall threw a hand up in frustration. "Just how many times do you have to flash the paparazzi before you start wearing underwear, huh? It's not rocket science, for fuck's sake. And she completely ignored the script I gave her and said, on camera, that she didn't usually participate in children's charities because kids are gross. She said the sick kids in the cancer ward were gross, Ray. How am I supposed to spin *that*? She *is* a brainless twatwaffle." She sniffed indignantly. "It's just my unfortunate luck that I said it within earshot of so many hot mics. It was an honest mistake that could've happened to anyone."

"Agreed. But that doesn't make you any less fired. Anyhoo, I'm bored with feeling sorry for you. Let's talk about me."

She blinked. That was abrupt, even for Ray, who was *not* known for his tact. "Wow, thanks for the sympathy, pal. You'd think that losing a boyfriend, my career, and my townhouse in one day would earn me the right to *wallow* at least a little."

Ray made a disgusted sound. "Kyle was a shitty boyfriend with a tiny dick who cleared his throat every eighteen seconds and said 'irregardless.' No loss there. And you'll have another job before this phone call is over."

She frowned. "Once and for all, Ray, I'm not going to dress up like Betty Draper and pretend I'm your secretary."

He scoffed. "No, silly. I mean a *real* job. Although I don't know what you have against *Mad Men.* You'd look just like January Jones all dolled up in a flouncy little skirt."

She was *so* not going to have this conversation with him today. "What job?"

Ray took a big dramatic breath. "I'm about to tell you something I've never told anyone in LA."

Anyone who didn't know Ray would probably be intrigued by the gravity of his tone. But Kendall knew him better than that. "Is this about the time you saw Ashton Kutcher at Starbucks?"

A pregnant pause on his end was followed by, "Dumbass, I told *everyone* that. I *said* I was going to tell you something I've never told anyone in LA."

True enough. She'd heard the Ashton Kutcher story at least twelve times. "OK, so spill."

"I have a brother."

"Great. Is he blond and single?"

She heard him slap a palm to his forehead. "Damn it, Kenny, I'm serious."

So was she. At least a little bit.

Ray then said the magic words. "He was a *bit* famous a few years ago."

Kendall leaned forward, suddenly *very* serious. "Why am I just now hearing about this?"

"Because I've seen you go after celebrities and it's like watching the shark swallow that little boy in *Jaws*. And he wasn't ready to be in the limelight again. If you'd convinced him to hire you when we first met, today he'd be the biggest name in the business, because you're incapable of half-assing anything. And he just wasn't ready."

"But he's ready now? So, what, is he some kind of washed-up child star looking to make a comeback?"

Kendall practically salivated at the thought. Washed up child stars were her specialty. If she'd been around to convince David Cassidy to sign with her, he would've had his own number-one-rated reality series or been the host of a top-tier talent competition instead of that Vegas residency he did.

"No. And I'm not telling you anything else. Not yet, anyway. I want you to meet him before you make any snap judgments."

She pursed her lips in frustration. "I don't make snap judgments."

"Puh-lease. You're Snappy McSnaperson, mayor of Snappytown."

"Well, that's just childish." A little true, too. Not that she'd admit that to *him*. "You have to give me something here, Ray. How do you even know I'll want to work with him after I've met him?"

"One, you love a challenge like no one I've ever seen in my life. And two, you don't have a choice, Kenny. You have posh taste, high-maintenance hair, and a shoe fetish. You *need* the job. Plus, you have little-to-no savings."

"How do you know I have little-to-no savings?"

He snorted. "Hel-lo? Not only am I a CPA, I'm *your* CPA. Did you forget that? So, unless you have an account in the Caymans I'm not aware of, you're damn near broke."

"It's not like I blew all my money on hair product and shoes, you know," she grumbled.

"I know, I know. You paid off your student loans and your parent's house like a good little girl. Oh, come on, sweetie. What do you have to lose?"

Thanks to Kyle, a whole helluva lot of nothing. Her name would be shit in this town by tomorrow. If it wasn't already. "Tell me this mystery brother doesn't already have an agent, and isn't in LA," she said.

"No agent. And he is hell-and-gone from LA."

And he was Ray's brother, so chances were good that he was a blond, not some hot, dark-haired, alpha jerkwad that'd be her Kryptonite. Again. A blond paying client who wasn't in LA sounded pretty really good right about now.

Besides, she hadn't met a client yet she couldn't handle. Drug addicts, sex scandals, has-beens and never-were's—she was a publicity *goddess* who could deal with them all.

How bad could it be?

Keep reading for a sneak peak into
Semi-Charmed

HARPER HALL
INVESTIGATIONS
BOOK 1

SEMI - CHARMED

ISABEL JORDAN

*She's infamous. He's legendary. Together, they'll be epic...or
a complete train wreck. It could go either way, really...*

CHAPTER 1

Whispering Hope, New York, today

Harper Hall swatted the fast-fingered hand of yet another horny, middle-aged CPA off her ass, but resisted the urge to dump tequila in this one's lap. After all, the Prince Valiant haircut and underbite he was saddled with were punishments enough for his crimes.

"Hey, baby," Valiant's friend said as he fondled his shot glass suggestively. "Is that a mirror in your pocket? 'Cause I can definitely see myself in your pants."

Harper rolled her eyes and shot back, "Darlin', I'm not your type. I'm not inflatable."

And with that, she turned on the heel of one of her requisite six-inch platforms and started for the bar as the CPAs chortled and bumped knuckles. They were probably looking at her butt too, but Harper chose not to dwell on that, or on the fact that most of said butt was probably hanging out of her Daisy Dukes. Not her best look, to be sure.

Lanie Cale, one of the other waitresses, grabbed her arm and leaned in, shouting over the music, "Hey, can you take over for me with the guy at table five? Carlos is letting me dance tonight. I go on in ten."

Harper gave her a quick once over. Lanie was five years her junior, ten pounds lighter, and had her beat by a full cup size. If she was Lanie, she'd probably aspire to be a stripper too. But as it stood, she was stuck waiting tables with the other B-cups.

"Sure," she answered. "But, Lanie, this guy at table five...he's not a CPA, is he? I don't think I have the strength for another CPA."

"No *way* is this guy a CPA. I'd bet Hugh Jackman's abs on it," she promised solemnly as she disappeared into the crowd.

At that moment, the sweaty throng of dancers and customers and waitresses parted, giving Harper her first glimpse of the guy at table five.

Wow. Hugh Jackman's abs were in no danger tonight.

The guy at table five was definitely *not* an accountant. Serial killer, maybe. CPA...um, no.

Table five was wedged in the corner, to the *extreme* right of the stage, which was why no one usually wanted to sit there. But instinct told Harper this guy had refused to sit anywhere else. This was one of those never-let-anyone-sneak-up-behind-you types, maybe with a military or law enforcement background. Paranoid and probably with good reason.

Everything about him screamed tall, dark, and brooding. From the black hair long overdue for a trim to the black-on-black wardrobe, complete with biker boots and a *Highlander*-like leather trench, this guy was either a true rebel without a cause, or the best imitation of one she'd ever seen.

And he was drunk off his ass. Not the kind of happy, silly drunk the CPAs at table ten had going. No, Harper could tell by the way he was ignoring the half-naked dancer on stage that he was drowning his sorrows.

Ignoring Misty Mountains wasn't easy, either. Her brand new double D's were mesmerizing, and the nipples kind of followed you wherever you went like the eyes on the creepy Jesus picture in her mom's living room.

As Harper watched, he polished off a bottle of Glenlivet and set it beside two other empties. She sighed. He'd probably pass out before he remembered to tip her. God damn drunks would be the death of her.

Harper squared her shoulders and walked up to the table, then knelt beside him so he could hear her over the bassline of Bon Jovi's *Lay Your Hands On Me*.

"Can I get you anything else, sir? Like coffee?" *Hint, hint.*

He didn't even glance at her as he slid the empty bottles to the edge of the table and said, "Another bottle."

His voice sent a shiver down her spine. It was gravelly, raspy, almost like he'd growled the words instead of speaking them. *Sexy.*

But sexy voice or not, she wasn't about to serve him another bottle. He was probably a few inches over six feet and maybe a little over two-hundred pounds, but no one—not even a manly man like this one—could down four bottles of eighteen-year-old Glenlivet and blow a Breathalyzer that wouldn't get him immediately arrested.

"I think you've probably had enough for tonight."

He slowly glanced over at her as if he hadn't really noticed her presence until just then. When her eyes locked with his, she completely forgot what they'd been talking about. Hell, who was she kidding? She forgot how to *breathe.*

This had to be the most gorgeous potential serial killer she'd ever seen.

He had a dark olive complexion most women would kill for, cheekbones sharp enough to cut glass, and eyes that were either black or the deepest blue she'd ever seen—it was too dark in the club to tell for sure.

His perfectly arched black brows—and they had to be naturally perfect, because she was pretty sure this guy wouldn't be caught dead waxing—raised sardonically as his gaze moved over her.

Harper fought the urge to suck in her stomach and desperately wished her uniform was a size eight instead of a four. She had dignity in a size eight. Class, even. In a four...not so much.

He lowered his gaze to her chest, and then slowly lifted it back to her eyes. "I doubt they're paying you to think, sunshine." Sliding the empty bottles even closer to her, he repeated, "Another bottle."

He'd said it very slowly, deliberately, in a manner most people reserved for slow-witted children and foreigners. The only part of her that wasn't at all impressed with the guy's fallen-angel face—which just happened to be her Sicilian temper—kicked in at that point.

Harper straightened and snagged the bottles off the table, preparing to verbally flay him, but just when she'd figured out exactly how many four-letter words she could hurl at him in one sentence, a premonition hit her hard.

People often asked her what premonitions felt like. Imagine someone punching a hole through your forehead and making a fist around your brain, she always told them. This premonition was no different.

Harper staggered forward and planted one palm on the table to steady herself as images assailed her: a young, blonde woman in an alley pinned to a dumpster by a man twice her size.

A vampire, she knew instinctively. Cold chills always shot down her spine when she saw them.

Harper sucked in a deep breath and forced herself to concentrate on details other than the victim, just like Sentry taught her so many years ago. Instead, she tried to picture the dumpster, the buildings around it, street signs…anything that might tell her where this girl was so she could call the police and get her some help.

And then she saw a logo printed on the side of the dumpster as big as life. *Kitty Kat Palace*.

Holy shit, the vamp and his victim were *here*.

Keep reading for a sneak peak into
Caped and Dangerous

Being a superhero is not all it's cracked up to be...

CHAPTER 1

Being a superhero is *not* all it's cracked up to be.

Evil doesn't take a break because you have a date, or the flu, or just *really* want to stay home and binge-watch *Supernatural* on Netflix while wearing slouchy socks and sweatpants.

Nope. Superheroes don't get vacation days. You're pretty much on call 24-7, with crappy state-employee health benefits and damn near useless dental coverage.

And for what? The feel-good knowledge that you're doing something good for your fellow man? The adoration of the public? *Pfffttt.* Sometimes the "adoring public" sues you because when you flew in to save them from a carjacking, you accidentally shattered their windshield with the bad guy's head.

A thank-you would be customary in such situations, but it doesn't happen as often as one would think.

And you know what else? Capes chafe the back of your neck like a *bitch.* They always feel like an irritating tag in the back of a $2 T-shirt.

These were all things Greer Glenanne, aka G-Force (a

stupid nickname she did *not* choose for herself, mind you), wished someone had told her *before* she'd taken the gig as the official superhero for Gem City.

But that was twenty-ish years ago. Back when she was shiny and new and so idealistic it *hurt*. There'd been so many things she'd wanted to do, so many people she'd wanted to help. She'd been so *sure* she would save the world one day.

Now she got sued by the people she saved. (Yeah…that was a true story, sadly.) Her bum knee ached so badly every time it rained she was forced to limp on the job. Sometimes she woke up and her back hurt for no reason at all. Or she threw it out entirely because she sneezed wrong.

As it turned out, being able to fly and bench press a Buick didn't protect you from all the typical middle-aged maladies that impacted normal folks.

Then there was the fact that she was in early onset menopause. That was a fun one. Hot flashes and heightened emotions. Just what every woman with superpowers should have.

So, if being a superhero sucked, being a *middle-aged* super-hero sucked the biggest bag of dicks the world had ever known.

"Hey! Yo, G!"

Greer startled at the voice that popped into her ear, nearly causing her to spill the mug of hot chocolate she'd just pulled out of her microwave.

Yeah. That was *another* thing that sucked about being a superhero. The Bluetooth-enabled cochlear implant that allowed her team to reach her, anytime, anywhere.

Day. Or. Night.

The sheer number of times she'd taken calls while on the toilet was appalling.

"What?" she snapped, wishing more than anything that she

could just drink her damn hot chocolate and go to bed. But Rio only said *"Yo"* in that tone when she wasn't going to like what he had to say.

Rio Flores was her tech support, her project manager, her personal assistant, and her best friend all rolled into one six-foot-tall, ridiculously attractive gay man who had better style than all the *Queer Eye* guys combined. He was her Overwatch—the Felicity Smoak to her Green Arrow.

And he was about to ruin her night. She could just feel it, from the tips of her messy bun to the soles of her fuzzy pink bunny slippers.

"I got a call from Hottie McStudly, my friend."

Greer groaned and squeezed her eyes shut. "Ugh. Not again. Please, don't tell me."

"OK. But he says he has something of yours. Again."

She pinched the bridge of her nose. "See, I *told* you not to tell me."

"Sorry," Rio said, not sounding sorry at all. "But we don't know for *sure* it's her this time."

Oh, of *course* it was her. It was *always* her. "Don't patronize me."

Bryn Terrell—no official superhero nickname yet—was and had always been a pain in the ass, ever since the state made her Greer's trainee.

It wasn't that Bryn was bad at the job. Quite the opposite, really. She was just *overzealous*. She tended to treat jaywalkers with the same "I am Justice" attitude she threw at bank robbers and muggers. She saw every petty thief and minor league crook in the state as *evil*. Greer had been at the superhero gig long enough to recognize all the shades of gray between good and evil.

There were *so* many shades of gray.

And Bryn's righteous quest for justice was topped off with a mountain of blonde curls, perky, 20-year-old boobs, and a sweet, lilting voice. All of that made Bryn almost more than Greer could take on a good day.

And today was *not* a good day.

Bryn had, for some reason, made it her life's mission to take down Killian Morgan, who Rio lovingly (or lustingly) referred to as Hottie McStudly.

About once a month for the past two years or so, Bryn got caught breaking into Killian's billion-dollar, corporate high rise, looking for "evidence of wrongdoings", as she put it.

Greer wasn't entirely sure what Killian had done to make his millions, and she wasn't certain what his employees did in that lavishly appointed high rise of his. What she *did* know was that he was way too smart to have any "evidence of wrongdoings" laying out where Bryn could stumble upon it.

And it wasn't like Killian didn't *know* that Bryn had X-ray vision. If there was anything in the building that could incriminate him, she would've seen it. Then she would've gleefully reported it all to Greer in that annoyingly pretty voice of hers, and Greer would've gotten a migraine.

Greer was willing to admit that, on some level, it irked her that Bryn might be at least a little *right* about Killian. The odds that he was completely innocent were most likely not favorable. After all, were any hot billionaires under fifty *not* crooked as hell? Greer didn't see how they couldn't be.

But as far as Greer knew, whatever Killian was doing wasn't actively hurting anyone. If anything, he was probably guilty of a bunch of white-collar crimes and money-making schemes that Greer didn't give a crap about. And Bryn wasn't going to find evidence of any of *that* in his building, or she would've already.

So, here she was, again, in the position of going to the

Morgan Enterprises building, and being forced to sweet talk Killian Morgan into *not* pressing charges against her trainee.

Which left Greer in yet *another* uncomfortable position. Because as much as she tried to ignore it, Killian Morgan was wildly attractive. And she did mean *wildly*. Like, throw-him-down-and-mount-him-like-a-rutting-beast *wildly*. She couldn't afford to develop a crush on him or indulge in any flirting. She did *not* need a sexual harassment suit on her record.

Greer fanned her face. Great. Now she was having a hot flash. Just the *thought* of sexually harassing Killian gave her hot flashes. Fan-fucking-tastic.

"Kiss him 'hi' for me, G," Rio said.

Greer let out an unladylike snort. "Yeah, sure. I'll get right on that," she said, still fanning her face.

"Honey, if I was you, I would've got on *that* years ago. Now, go collect the B-Team."

"You know she hates it when you call her that."

"I could call her Plan B, if you'd prefer? Betamax?"

Even in her foul mood, Greer got a chuckle out of that. "You know I love you, right?"

"*Pfffttt*. Of course you do. Who else would pick up your hormones from the drugstore and iron your capes?

ABOUT THE AUTHOR

The normal:

Isabel Jordan writes because it's the only profession that allows her to express her natural sarcasm and not be fired. She is a paranormal and contemporary romance author. Isabel lives in the U.S. with her husband, her son, a neurotic shepherd mix, and a ginormous Great Dane mix named Jerkface (but don't feel bad for Jerkface. He's earned the name).

The weird:

Now that the normal stuff is out of the way, here's some weird-but-true facts that would never come up in polite conversation. Isabel Jordan:

1. Is terrified of butterflies (don't judge ... it's a real phobia called lepidopterophobia)
    2. Is a lover of all things ironic (hence the butterfly on the original cover of *Semi-Charmed*)
    3. Is obsessed with *Supernatural, Game of Thrones, The Walking Dead, The 100, Once Upon a Time,* and *Dog Whisperer.*
    4. Hates coffee. Drinks a Diet Mountain Dew every morning.
    5. Will argue to the death that *Pretty in Pink* ended all wrong.

(Seriously, she ends up with the guy who was embarrassed to be seen with her and not the nice guy who loved her all along? That would never fly in the world of romance novels.)

6. Would eat Mexican food every day if given the choice.

7. Reads two books a week in varied genres.

8. Refers to her Kindle as "the precious."

9. Thinks puppy breath is one of the best smells in the world.

10. Is a social media idgit. (Her husband had to explain to her what the point of Twitter was. She's still a little fuzzy on what Instagram and Pinterest do.)

11. Kicks ass at Six Degrees of Kevin Bacon.

12. Stole her tagline idea ("weird and proud") from her son. Her tagline idea was, "Never wrong, not quite right." She liked her son's idea better.

13. Breaks one vacuum cleaner a year because she ignores standard maintenance procedures (Really, you're supposed to empty the canister every time you vacuum? Does that seem excessive to anyone else?)

14. Is still mad at the WB network for cancelling *Angel* in 2004.

15. Can't find her way from her bed to her bathroom without her glasses, but refused eye surgery, even when someone else offered to pay. (They lost her at "eye flap". Seriously, look it up. Scary stuff.)